TIPPER LAKE

A Tyler Monroe Mystery

W. Thomas Geer

ISBN: **1535186704**
ISBN: 9781535186704

DEDICATION

Dedicated to the memory of our daughter, Sarita Wright Lucas and granddaughter Clare Lucas. They will forever remain in our family's hearts and mind. Please take a moment to visit www.saritaandclairefoundation.org

CHAPTER ONE

"I know you in there, so for the love of Christ get your ass up. We got work to do young man. Hear what I'm saying?" His high-pitched voice was just as annoying as the relentless pounding on the door.

I buried my head under a second pillow to drown out the racket. It was wishful thinking on my part, but I hoped he might give up if I could only bear the noise a little longer. I glanced at the clock on the nightstand. It was 5am on a Sunday morning. Such is the life of a detective.

"Monroe, open up. Don't go playing dumb with me, you hear?"

After savoring one last moment of comfortable bliss, I pulled back the sheets and sat up slowly, trying hard not to aggravate my lower back. To make matters worse, I had one hell of a hangover.

"Monroe!" he yelled again for what must have been the umpteenth time. Convinced he had no intention of leaving, and fully naked, I grabbed the edge of the nightstand, stood up and began my trek towards the door. Despite my lack of balance I survived, carefully stepping over the beer bottles and clothes scattered across the floor. I unlocked the door and opened it as far as the attached chain lock would permit, one hand covering my manhood.

"I guess persistence pays off doesn't it?" I hissed through the opening.

"Well for the love of Christ it's about time," Bobby yelled. "You know how long I been standing out here beating on this door?"

"In case you've forgotten, *it is Sunday*."

"Well *forgive me* if I interrupted your beauty sleep," he shot back, adjusting his belt and pulling up his sagging pants over his stomach. His favorite blue tie was missing, his shirt was only partially buttoned, and his grey gabardine suit was wrinkled. He looked stunned.

"Put cha clothes on. We got work to do. We gotta check out a murder up at Lakeside Estates," he said. He removed a crumpled white handkerchief from his back pocket and, with his hand slightly trembling, began wiping the sweat from his brow. His eyes were red and swollen.

I opened the door a little wider but still not enough for him to see inside. "A murder?"

"Yeah. Earl's dead," he responded quietly, looking down.

I stood speechless for a moment, trying to process what I thought I'd heard.

"Earl. You mean… Judge McKenna?"

"Yeah," he answered, shaking his head. "May God have mercy on his soul." He made the sign of the cross over his chest with his hand and removed his thick bi-focal glasses in order to catch small pockets of tears that had pooled in both eyes, about to spill down his cheeks.

"I'd known him all my life," he said sadly. "We practically grew up together right here in Savannah. I was his best man when he married Sue Ellen. I still can't believe it.

"What the hell happened?" I demanded.

"Don't know at the moment, but from what I was told, there was a three alarm fire at his home north of the city. Body was found in the bedroom."

"What makes you think he was murdered?" I asked. He hesitated for a moment before answering.

"I don't know," he answered finally, shaking his head. "I can't explain it, but I got a strange feeling about it." He reached into his coat pocket, and then fitted a hearing aid to his left ear before continuing. "A man in his position is bound to have enemies. It's the nature of his job."

"Yeah…I suppose so. Any suspects?"

He shook his head, no. "I don't know much at this point but the Chief wants all hands on deck so we better get. Understand?"

"I'll meet you at the car outside. This place is a real mess."

"Yeah, it smells like a sewer out here," he said as I closed the door.

I had lost count of the times I had been lectured about the smelly hall outside my apartment.

I headed back to the bedroom, carefully making my way around clothes and empty beer bottles. I'd never been big on cleaning, particularly after working twelve–hour days. Moving boxes were still stacked everywhere, even though I'd been living in this shit-hole for six months. Hopefully my deal with the Feds would come to an end soon, but for now, as long as I could find everything I needed, I didn't consider the untidiness a big deal.

I took a quick shower, put on a clean white shirt and grabbed the first tie I could find. With any luck they would match the dark colored pants and the light cotton sport jacket hanging in the back of the closet. Being colorblind required me to have a system of identifying clothes to avoid mismatches - BU for blue, GR – green, GY for grey, etc. The system helped but provided no excuse for plain old bad taste.

I skipped shaving and grabbed the .38 under my pillow. Sleeping with a loaded .38 felt a bit paranoid, but I'd learned from my past to keep my piece close by at all times. As always, my adrenalin rose as I checked the barrel and placed it in its holster under my coat. *Hallelujah, finally a chance to do some real goddamn detective work.* This could be the break I'd been waiting for. Six months of petty burglaries, storefront robberies, and missing people had worn my patience thin. It was too damn bad it had to happen this way.

By now the sunrise was starting to peek through the partially drawn venetian blinds as I quietly headed for the front door. Even at this hour it was obvious that today would be another long hot miserable August day. The early morning sounds of roosters crowing and milk trucks making deliveries were a continual reminder that this was the Deep South and not Brooklyn.

I washed down a handful of aspirin with the remains of last night's Jack Daniels and tossed the bottle in the overflowing trashcan in the living room. I quietly closed the bedroom door after turning around to take one last look. Amazingly she had slept through all the noise and commotion. I guess it had been one hell of a night.

Earl McKenna or "the Judge" as the locals called him, was a prominent figure in Savannah who had served as the city's Chief Judge for the past twelve years. He had deep political ties and regularly rubbed elbows with the wealthy and elite in Savannah and Chatham County. Some said he had his sights set on the governor's office one day. His wife Sue Ellen was your typical suburban politician's wife, known for hosting lavish tea parties and political fundraisers. On the surface they appeared to be a perfect couple, but things aren't always what they appear to be.

On the drive up to the crime scene none of the local radio stations made any mention of the fire. Apparently the press hadn't gotten word of anything yet. The big news on all the stations this morning was the ongoing drama between JFK and the Soviets.

Seemed as though the whole world was waiting nervously to see how Kennedy would respond to the missiles the commies had put in Cuba. In all my twenty-nine years, I'd never witnessed *anything* as scary as this. Hopefully cooler heads would prevail and the situation would find a peaceful resolution, but only time would tell. Unable to find any news about the fire, I turned to a blues station, turned up the volume, and lit a Marlboro.

"Nothing on the radio. Seems like word hasn't gotten out yet. Don't you think that's strange considering a man of his stature?" I asked my partner, taking a nice long drag.

"You know you need to cut that out, don't ya," Bobby replied, ignoring my question.

I pulled out the metal ashtray next to the radio and dropped a few ashes inside. "It's a cigarette. What's the big deal? Never killed anybody."

"I ain't talking about that," he answered keeping both hands on the steering wheel and looking straight ahead. "If you wanna smoke that's your business. I'm talking bout that *other* stuff."

"Other stuff? What other stuff?" I asked, playing dumb just to irritate him.

He took his eyes off the road long enough to turn off the radio.

"Look-a-here. Don't you start with me, boy. You know exactly what I'm talking about. It's *six o'clock in the morning* for Christ sake. Don't you think it's a little too early to be drinking from the Devil's bottle? If I can smell it, don't you think everybody else can too? Don't you know the Bible says that drunkards shall not inherit the kingdom of God?"

I sat there silently not really sure how to respond – or if *I* even *wanted to.* It certainly wasn't the first time we'd had this conversation. I knew he meant well but old habits were hard to break. This damn city—its people and the slow pace of life—certainly didn't help the situation either. Transferring to Savannah from New York had been tougher than I had imagined. It certainly wasn't a move I wanted to make and Jack Daniels had helped ease the transition. Like an old friend, JD was always there to keep the demons at bay.

"You know I like you, Monroe," Bobby started up again, after it became obvious to him that I had no intention of responding. "Chief likes you too. Now I don't know why you transferred down here from New York City. Maybe that ain't none of my business, but I believe you got real potential Youngblood. I'd just hate to see you mess up over something stupid like this. You got to remember that this isn't New York. This here's a country town where *everybody* knows *everybody.* Now what you do off duty is your business, but you can't be doing that on the job. You understand?" He paused for a moment before turning the radio back on and pushing the preset button for his country station.

"The invitation's still open every Thursday night up at White Rock Church if you need to talk to somebody about that...problem."

"Whatever," I replied, taking another drag.

"And while we on the subject of getting your act together, that hair's gotten a little long, don't ya think? You need to do something bout that mop. Pretty soon you'll be looking like one of them rock and roll musicians all the kids been going crazy over," he chuckled.

"What you *need* to do is go see Delroy. Now I don't know how you feel about going over to the colored side of town, but that colored boy sho' can cut some hair. It'll set you back a buck fifty but I'll tell you what, it's worth *every* penny."

I guess he had a point about the hair; it *was* getting a little long, but the church suggestion--not happening. Since arriving in Savannah he'd been hounding me about attending his Thursday night prayer meetings. I politely declined each time the subject came up. Church just wasn't my bag. To me it was just a bunch of con artists sucking money from naive followers in return for a weekly "dose of hope."

Without saying another word I switched the radio back to the blues station just in time to hear the last few stanzas of Muddy Waters' *Still a Fool.*

As the new guy in the department, I guess I'd pulled the short straw in the department's new "buddy" system. Bobby Lee was a thirty-year veteran who'd spent the last ten years in Savannah's Detective Bureau. He carried a couple hundred pounds on a five-foot frame and walked with a slight limp as a result of a battle with diabetes. While I had a penchant for nice Italian suits and fancy shoes, he wore the same grey polyester suit and blue tie every day. He was a devout Southern Baptist and I was a non-believer. Unsurprisingly, he found a way to interject every conversation with a Bible passage or verse. We were quite the odd couple to say the least.

But he was a good cop with less than a year before retirement. Truth be told, I envied the son-of-a-bitch. In addition to Almighty

Jesus, the only other interests he had were fishing and the boat he planned to buy when he retired--a 1957 Chris Craft Constellation with twin Chrysler V8 engines and a triple-axle trailer. Nice boat, but I'm not sure how he ever expected to buy something like that on a detective's salary. Maybe he had a side hustle. Who knows? Regardless, he was looking forward to that day. As a matter of fact, he'd even begun marking off the days on the Sears and Roebuck calendar that hung over the office water cooler. Until then, we'd been assigned to work together on local cases while I secretly pursued an undercover assignment for the Feds. We argued regularly, but always managed to respect one another. Hopefully our differences wouldn't get in the way of solving this crime.

By taking the dirt roads around Tipper Lake we were able to avoid the Sunday morning church traffic so our ride to Lakeside Estates was a short one. You'd never expect the murder of such a prominent figure to happen in a small backwoods city like Savannah. Nonetheless it presented a challenge and fortunately a welcome relief from the mundane work I'd been doing for the last six months.

CHAPTER TWO

A thick layer of smoke cast a gloomy brown haze over the entire lake front community ten miles north of Savannah. It had been one hell of a fire at the Judge's house. The smell combined with the early morning heat and rising humidity guaranteed it would be another miserable day.

Lakeside Estates was clearly a community of "haves." Endless rows of large column front homes with perfectly manicured lawns and white picket fences lined the streets. Neighbors gathered on their front lawns as we drove by—curious, confused and undoubtedly shocked that something like this could happen in their quiet upper middle class sanctuary.

After following a procession of fire trucks, we stopped at a police detail, blocking access to what appeared to be the entrance to a private driveway. Not able to get any closer, we pulled over and parked next to a vintage 1950 baby blue Mercedes Benz Cabriolet with a white convertible top. I guessed that it had belonged to McKenna. I stopped for a moment to admire the one of a kind classic but the Benz didn't impress Bobby. He seemed more focused on something else as we got out of his vehicle.

"Looks like our boys are already on the scene." He pointed to a newer squad car parked to our left, referring to our office mates, Pete and Andy. As the department's veteran detectives, they typically got first dibs on all the major cases. This investigation had just taken a turn for the worst with these two on the scene.

At six foot five, fiftyish and balding, Pete Krasner was the senior of the two partners, with over twenty years on the force. His questionable interrogating tactics and intense dislike for colored folk had earned him a reputation for ruthlessness within the department and the community. Andy Reed or "Reebo" was a Korean War vet, a loose cannon with a quick trigger finger. Like me, he was a chain smoker who couldn't seem to kick the habit. Neither fit the image of what one would expect to be Savannah's finest. Actually they looked more like a redneck version of Abbott and Costello.

We were colleagues, but not very hospitable toward each other. Having to share a cramped office with these two meant witnessing both their casual incompetence and their blatant disrespect for Negro people. They were nothing more than two thugs hiding behind badges. The likelihood of having to work with these two idiots on this case was starting to crush my earlier enthusiasm. But, despite the mutual dislike, we still had a job to do. I continued up the winding driveway, unable to avoid the two on their way back down.

"Now you play nice you hear?" Bobby whispered, giving me a hard stare as they approached. "I mean it. We don't need any trouble today."

"Well I'll be damned…if it ain't *Big City* and the old man!" Pete smirked, stopping to look me up and down before turning his head to the side to spit out a wad of chewing tobacco. "You boys sure you in the right place?" He wiped the corner of his mouth with the back of his hand and removed his straw hat to fan the sweat on his forehead. "This ain't no nigger purse snatching you know."

"Hell, that ain't their beat anyhow," piped in his partner Andy.

"Yeah, you right," Pete chuckled. "I forgot you boys get all the "special" assignments. I bet y'all on the trail of them missing dogs ain't ya? If memory serves me right, I think you want the next town over, ain't that right Andy?" he asked, looking back at his partner with a smile.

"That's what I heard," Andy answered. "If I was you I'd be real careful too. That's a pretty ornery bunch from what I heard. You got your rabies shots?"

"We got everything under control here," Pete announced. "Why don't you two amateurs leave this here police work to a couple of *real* detectives?"

Real detectives?

I could understand their lack of respect for me. Personally I didn't give a damn, but I bristled at them disrespecting a twenty-year veteran. I was tempted to ignore Bobby's suggestion to play nice, but finally simply smiled and flipped them both the finger as we passed by each other. Bobby grinned next to me.

"Hey Fancy Pants. Tell me something," Pete yelled as we continued up the driveway. "Where can I get me some of them nigger shoes like the ones you got on? Hell, I hear shoes like that make you dance real smooth." I'd grabbed the first pair of shoes I could find in my rush out the door this morning—my black and white Stacy Adams wingtips. I typically wore them with my double-breasted plaid suit on Friday nights. I may not have admired much about my father, but I did admire the man's taste in shoes.

"Couldn't find ya big boy shoes this morning?" Andy smirked. "I bet them niggers taught you how to tap dance when you bought them shoes too, didn't they? Come on Junior, show us what you learned" He laughed and attempted to do a little jig.

Against my better judgment, I stopped, took a deep breath and turned around.

"Living down here in the Deep South, I wouldn't expect you to know anything about *real* shoes, seeing as though you rednecks are probably used to running around barefoot." Bobby sighed and shook his head in disbelief. I dropped the Marlboro I had lit just a moment ago and stepped on it before continuing.

"Yeah, I guess they are a little too fancy for work, aren't they? Typically I wouldn't wear these shoes on a day like today, but on my way out this morning I couldn't seem to find the ones I normally wear. For the life of me, I just can't remember *where* I left my shoes last night." Pete turned to Andy with a confused look on his face. "But I'd really appreciate it if you'd check with your wife. I think she might know."

"You mother…"Pete tossed his straw hat on the ground and stormed up the driveway in my direction like a madman. For a split second, seeing that big six-foot frame charging in my direction gave me second thoughts about the trouble my mouth had just gotten my ass into. Nonetheless, I needed to put an end to all the harassment once and for all. These two had been on my case since I'd arrived. I know Bobby wouldn't understand, but it was all about respect. Besides, Pete wouldn't be the first ass I'd kicked.

"You '*bout* to get a Georgia style ass whipping City Boy," he growled, a stench of chewing tobacco on his breath; we now stood toe to toe. I kept silent to keep him from smelling the JD on *my* breath.

"Hell yeah! Teach Mr. Fancy Pants here a lesson," yelled Andy, grinning like a little kid bout to watch a schoolyard fight. "Show 'em how we do it down home."

"I got this," Pete replied, flashing a slight grin.

Joe Louis once said *everyone has a plan until they've been hit.*

We stood there waiting for the other to make the first move. His eyes constantly shifted from right to left, but never making any direct contact with mine.

"For the love of Christ, the two of you's need to quit acting like little kids!" hollered Bobby, forcing his way between the two of us. "We got a murder on our hands and y'all acting like a bunch of third-graders. Now cut it out you hear me?" He looked at me with disappointment. "You in particular need to let this go," he warned, pointing his finger in my face.

"This ain't over," Pete said, smiling and stepping back. Still standing behind Pete, Andy made a choking gesture with both hands around his neck.

"You know where to find me…and don't forget to bring your little bitch with you," I hollered as Bobby pushed me away.

"Who you calling a bitch? Boy don't you know I'll kick yo Yankee…"

"And what the hell's going on over here?" yelled a familiar figure coming from our right, wearing plaid golf shorts and white golf shoes. Behind him was a collection of firemen, police officers and reporters with tape recorders slung over their shoulders. It was rather unusual to see Chief Davis at this point in an investigation, although it made sense considering the high profile nature of the investigation.

"No problem here Chief," a visibly nervous Bobby answered. "Just a slight misunderstanding that's all. We're on it boss."

"Well you damn well better be!" he said, fidgeting with one side of his waxed handle bar mustache. "This is a real *serious* situation here." He paused for a moment, scanning the cordoned off area for a private place to talk, away from the crowd following him.

He pointed to a vacant area near the fire trucks before turning around to address the people behind him. They immediately began shouting questions.

"Now everybody just *calm down, all right*?" he yelled. He stood silently for a moment, waiting for them to comply.

"Right now we don't have much of anything to report," he began, speaking into a throng of microphones and cameras shoved in his face by reporters pushing and elbowing to get closer. "The investigation is ongoing. We'll provide a statement the minute we have something substantial to report. That's all for now."

"Is that it?" yelled a reporter in the rear of the crowd.

"That's all I got right now," he answered.

"Was the cause of death a homicide or was it fire related?" asked another reporter. "We heard there were shots fired."

"At this point nothing has been confirmed, so I'd advise you not to speculate. Do I make myself clear?" he asked before walking away from the crowd and signaling us to follow. Several police officers quickly formed a human barrier separating us from the crowd, as we followed him to a roped off area at the bottom of the driveway.

"I guess you know this is pretty big news," he sighed. He took off his golf cap after removing the glove on his right hand and placing both in his back pocket. He wiped the sweat from his forehead with a handkerchief while the four of us waited patiently waited for him to continue.

"The governor and the mayor are all over my ass so I need answers and I need 'em pretty goddamn quick. Anyone here *not* understand what I'm saying?" he asked in a low and commanding voice. No one said a word.

"What's the latest?" I asked finally.

"From what we can tell so far, it definitely looks like a homicide, but we don't have a suspect. Keep that under your hat. If the press finds out, it'll be a goddamn circus! The mayor has asked us to enforce a news blackout until further notice. That means don't say nothing to nobody. Nothing, understand?" He looked us straight in the face with his piercing blue eyes. That would explain why there had been no mention of the homicide on the radio on the drive up this morning.

"What about clues?" I asked.

"We've collected some evidence, but nothing conclusive," he answered nervously, pulling on the bright red suspenders holding up his golf shorts. "In the meantime we've taken the judge's wife downtown for questioning and to have her checked out by a physician."

"As a suspect or victim?" I asked curiously.

"Who knows? At this point we can't rule anything out. What I need you boys to do is talk to family, friends, neighbors…any goddamn person that might have a connection to McKenna. You know the drill. I'm sure a man in his position had enemies, shady business deals and Lord knows what else was going on, so get out there and see what you can dig up. Just don't talk to any reporters. Leave that to me. I'll make an official statement to the press later today. Everybody understand?"

We all nodded in agreement. He put on his golf cap and quickly made his way back up the driveway, avoiding the attention of a group of reporters heading in his direction. While Pete and Andy headed back to the office, we decided to ignore the boss's orders and stick around a little longer to see what we could learn. We agreed to split up, with Bobby speaking to a few of his press contacts on the scene while I examined what remained of the smoldering two-story. An analysis of the crime scene would give me an opportunity to look for clues and perhaps any additional evidence that might have been overlooked by Pete and Andy.

CHAPTER THREE

I cautiously entered the smoke filled two-story house after showing my badge to the officer at the entrance to the home. At least an inch of water covered the wood flooring and several windows had been shattered, most likely to release smoke that still lingered inside. I began my inspection one room at a time, covering my mouth and nose with a handkerchief, being careful not to disturb any crime scene evidence.

It was a traditional Southern column-front mansion, maybe a hundred years old or more. The first floor was badly damaged but looked structurally intact, most likely due to the quality of its turn of the century construction.

Most of the furniture scattered about had been damaged by fire or water used to extinguish the fire. In some cases both. A large area rug in the main living room had been pulled back from the floor in several sections, exposing burn patterns on the wood floor beneath. The baseboard molding and walls also had charred burn patterns, confirming that some type of flammable liquid had been splashed on them - most likely gasoline. I'd seen similar evidence when I'd investigated mob extortions in New York. A lab analysis would corroborate my assumption, but then again this was the Savannah PD and not the NYPD. Trusting my instincts, I cut out a small section of burnt carpet with my pocketknife and stuck it in my back pocket.

It had all the classic signs of arson. Add a dead body into the mix and you had the perfect set-up for a murder. Assuming that to be the case, where then was the body found? That's a key piece of information that would drive the search for clues. We had arrived too late to actually see the victim and there were no crime scene markings anywhere on this floor. That would most likely mean the body was found somewhere upstairs.

I continued my investigation for another half hour or so, stopping occasionally to scribble a few notes in a small red spiral notebook. Satisfied with my inspection of the main floor, I headed upstairs, carefully examining each step of the winding staircase for signs of burn patterns or gasoline splatters.

"Hey Tyler…you in here?" Bobby called.

"Yeah, up here," I answered, leaning over the railing at the top of the stairs and looking down. "Did you get any info?"

"Hold on a second." He adjusted the hearing aid that had slipped out of his left ear.

"Say what now?" he asked.

"What did you find out?"

"Not much," he yelled. "Nobody seems to know anything."

"What about the body?" I asked. He was still fumbling with the aid.

"The what?"

"The *body?*" I repeated, this time louder.

"Oh, the body. In the master bedroom," he yelled, finally getting it back in correctly. He slung a large Polaroid camera over his shoulder and began carefully making his way across the water-soaked floor towards the staircase.

I suggested we split up in order to cover more ground faster. I pointed to my left as he reached the top of the stairs. "See what you can find on that side and I'll check out the rooms over here." He gave me the thumbs up and headed in that direction.

I began my trek toward the right side, down the hall, carefully stepping over puddles before stopping at the entrance to a small room. There was considerably less fire damage on this floor. That could possibly mean the fire department had arrived in time to contain the fire before it had completely destroyed this floor of the house. A white canopy bed mostly covered in gray ash stood in the center of the room. Brightly colored wallpaper had peeled off the walls. A fancy dollhouse turned on its side had been pushed into a corner with several antique dolls by its side. It was obviously a young girl's room.

"Over here!" yelled Bobby from the other side of the hall as I began a closer look inside the small room. "Tyler. Take a look at this."

I made a few notes and carefully stepped around a few items in my path before meeting him on the other side of the stairway.

"Take a look at this," he said, handing me a small silver medallion about the size of a quarter. It had an impression of Saint Peter the Apostle.

"What's the big deal?"

"Take a look at the other side," he answered. I turned it over to find an inscription. *I will always love you--KJ.*

"Where'd you find this?

"Right here he answered, pointing to a location in front of the bedroom door.

"Looks like it might belong to a necklace. Any sign of that?"

"Nope. Looked all over," Bobby answered. "Maybe the crime scene crew found it." I held it up to get a better look, turned it on its side and examined the edges.

"Any idea who KJ might be?" I asked, placing the medallion in my coat pocket. He stared at me for a moment and then shook his head.

"You *do know* that's crime scene evidence right?"

"Any idea where the body was found?" I asked, ignoring his question and entering the bedroom. Unlike the small room on the other side, there was considerable fire damage in this room and the carpet on the floor was soaked with water.

"The body?" I repeated as he stood silently staring at a picture in a beautiful hand carved wooden frame hanging on the wall.

"I remember that day like it was yesterday," he said sadly. "That's Sue Ellen right there." He pointed to the woman in a flowing white gown. "What a beautiful bride she was. You see that little fella on the right there with the curly hair? That's my boy. I guess it's true what they say, ain't it? Tomorrow's not promised to anyone." I couldn't recall him ever mentioning a son before. I was curious, but decided now might not be a good time to open that door. He fell silent.

"According to one of my contacts, the body was found somewhere near the foot of the bed," he answered finally, pointing to an area to his left. "He was a good man. May the good Lord Almighty have mercy on his soul."

If in fact this had been a homicide, finding any traces of blood would be next to impossible with the amount of water covering the floor. Also, there were no apparent traces of blood on the bed or any visible signs of a struggle. Everything appeared to be intact.

I examined the charred remains of the bedroom door pulled off its hinges and leaning against the wall. It had no lock. Out of curiosity, I walked over to the only window in the bedroom, pulling it open with very little effort. Neither made sense to me.

"What you thinking?" he asked, sensing that I was on to something.

"This doesn't make any sense."

"How so?"

"No signs of a struggle and there's no lock on the door or the window. He could've easily escaped the fire. That only leaves one explanation."

"Which is?" he asked.

"How much would you say McKenna weighed?"

"Why is that important?" he asked.

"How much?" I repeated.

"Well… he was a pretty big boy," he answered. "I'd guess maybe 200 pounds."

"My thoughts exactly. You think you could carry someone that heavy up that spiral staircase?"

"Ain't no way."

"That means he was murdered somewhere on *this floor.* If that's the case, there's only one other place that could have happened." I scribbled a few notes in my spiral pad while he began taking photos with his Polaroid. We then headed over to the room on other side. Once there we began a sweep of the smaller room looking for any evidence that might indicate the actual spot of the homicide. Bobby took pictures from every corner of the room to construct a complete picture of the scene while I began examining the furniture and dolls scattered about the floor. Each doll was made of solid wood and a lot heavier than it appeared. They were exactly the same – long blonde hair, wearing white-laced camisole dresses. The only difference was the amount of soot on the dolls and their clothing. Some had very little, while others were completely covered. They also were soaking wet and had dark patches in their blonde hair…that is, all except one.

"Bobby. Take a look at this."

He stopped snapping photos, slung the camera around his neck and carefully stepped across the water soaked floor.

"They're all the same except this one. What's different?" I asked, handing him one of the dolls. He pulled up his pants at the knees and stooped down to study each of the dolls I had arranged on the wet floor before examining the one in his hand.

"I don't know much about dolls, but looks to me like this one's got the dress on backwards."

"Exactly. Certainly not a mistake a woman or a young girl would make."

"What color is McKenna's hair"? I asked.

"You seen McKenna before," he answered somewhat surprised, handing me back the doll. I *had* met McKenna several times, but when you're colorblind even hair color looks the same.

"Let me hold that pocket knife of yours."

He reached into his coat pocket pulled it out and tossed it to me. I used one of the smaller blades to separate a section of the doll's blond hair while he watched with curiosity. There were several dark stains on the side of this doll's head, which at first glance appeared to be ash. But one particular stain had a brighter, slightly different shade.

What's that look like?" I asked him, giving him the doll with a small patch of hair separated from the rest. He used a handkerchief to clean his glasses and carried it over to the window to get a better look.

"You thinking this might be blood?" he asked, wide-eyed and amazed.

"Certainly looks like that to me."

I removed a few strands of hair with stains and placed them in a handkerchief. Evidently the focus of the investigation had only been downstairs and across the hall, leaving this room unexamined. If in fact the murder had occurred in this room, then the overturned dollhouse and scattered furniture were likely the result of a struggle, and not the fire. It all began to make sense. McKenna was murdered with a wooden doll and dragged into the master bedroom. The fire, I assumed, was just a cover up—straight forward and simple.

A blow from a solid object that heavy would certainly leave more blood than was present—not only on the doll, but also on the floor and furniture. The only visible evidence of blood however was that small patch on the doll's hair. The doll with the dress on backwards was completely free of blood. So we were missing two key pieces of evidence – the bloody dress and the doll this clean dress came from.

The smart thing to do would be to get rid of both. When fear and adrenalin take over however, criminals don't always make the most logical decisions. If I were a betting man I'd say both the doll and the bloody dress were still somewhere in this house; the question was *where*? What had we missed?

"Give me a hand with this?" I asked, walking over and crouching down next to an overturned dollhouse in the corner. I grabbed one end of the roof and directed to him to grab the other end in order to turn it right side up.

"Just hold your end steady." I gave my end a hard tug, just enough to remove the entire piece. With the roof off, we were able to see inside from the top down, spotting a doll hidden inside a hollow section of the dollhouse. It had no dress. The fact that the clean dress on the murder weapon had been put on backwards meant the murderer was either in a hurry or he or she knew nothing about doll clothes…the latter not likely a mistake a woman would make.

Unfortunately, we were still missing the bloody dress.

"Okay, so now what?" Bobby asked.

Without saying a word, I gave him both dolls and left the room, heading for the staircase and down to the first floor. Curious, he followed close behind. We entered the remains of what appeared to have been the kitchen.

"This place is a mess," he said, carefully stepping around an overturned chair and a badly damaged table. "What you looking for down here?"

I released the latch at the top of a furnace door and began removing the burnt contents, placing each on a nearby counter. For the next half hour or so we closely examined the contents of the furnace item-by-item hoping to find anything potentially tied to the murder. I was close to giving up when I spotted something.

"What's that look like to you?" I asked lifting a small burnt fragment with a pencil. It appeared to be a small burnt patch of cloth, possibly the remains of a doll's dress. It also had noticeable traces of a brown stain that might be blood.

"Well I'll be a son of a gun. If that's what I think it is, then I guess your hunch was right, Monroe."

"Let's not celebrate just yet. If the lab can get some decent finger prints from these dolls *and* confirm the blood type from the hair stain and these fragments, *then* we might be on to something. Whoever did this did a good job of cleaning up the mess, but missed that one small spot in the hair. That's typical. They always miss *something*."

"But why bother switching the dress in the first place?" he asked. "That don't make any sense to me. Why not just burn the doll *and* the dress?

"We're dealing with an amateur that's why," I answered. "Most crimes of passion, if that's what this is, aren't planned. They're completely spontaneous."

"Crimes of what?"

"Crimes of passion," I repeated.

"That what they teach you in that fancy place, *what you call it* up North?"

"School of Criminology," I answered.

"Whatever. Assuming that's the case, what's our next move?" he asked, handing me the other burned fragment of cloth.

I stood up and brushed a spot of ash from the sleeve of my jacket. Looks like we had our murder weapon, but we still didn't have a motive.

"We need to get our hands on the suspect list Pete and Andy are putting together. We might find something there. I'm sure he's put a lot of people behind bars over the years."

"Don't you think we need to let the Chief in on what we've found first?" he asked.

"I suppose you're right, but nothing about the medallion... deal?"

"You *really* think that thing's got something to do with this?" he asked while closing the furnace door and locking it in place. I removed the medallion from my pocket and took another look, flipping it from side to side. There was something about it that just felt strange. I couldn't explain it. I put it back in my pocket.

"Maybe the murderer dropped it. Who knows? We can't rule anything out at this point, so for now, this stays between the two of us. Deal?"

He stared at me for a moment and shook his head as we walked towards the front entrance of the house.

I took his silence as a yes.

CHAPTER FOUR

The entrance to City Hall was mobbed with reporters and cameramen, all pushing and shoving for a chance to get any available updates on the investigation. The media circus was to be expected considering the high profile nature of the crime. Still, in my six months in the department I'd never seen anything like this. Bobby and I entered through the rear of the building to avoid the madness and took the freight elevator up to the second floor office we called home.

Originally an old storage room, the Detective Bureau consisted of a two small offices above City Hall. Bobby and I shared the front room with Pete and Andy, while the Chief occupied the back room. There were no windows and the only relief on a hot summer day came from a small rotating fan on top of an old metal file cabinet. It wasn't ideal, but was functional. As we walked in, Andy was searching through a stack of old newspapers and Pete's chair was empty. Even though the Chief's door was shut, you could still hear the muffled sound of voices inside.

"So who's in with the Chief?" asked Bobby, pushing aside a stack of case folders on his desk in order to see Andy.

He took a sip of coffee from an oversized mug before answering. "The DA, Mayor, and Medical Examiner."

"Really? What's happening?"

"They got a confession out of Sue Ellen," he said, smug. Bobby and I looked at each other, confused.

"You mean she confessed to the homicide?" he asked.

"Yeah" he gloated. "She confessed this morning. She's being booked on premeditated murder. The Medical Examiner confirmed multiple blows to the head as the primary cause of death."

"And the fire?"

"It was all a cover up."

"Well what about the murder weapon?"

"They believe it was destroyed in the fire."

"Well… I guess that makes it an open and shut case," said Bobby, staring directly at me, perplexed.

"Yeah, sure does look that way don't it? What you got there?" Andy asked. "Dog bones?"

"Oh, just something I need to take back to the store after lunch" Bobby answered, shoving the bag further under his arm and out of sight.

"So where's Sue Ellen now?" I asked.

"She's being questioned by Pete. She waived her right to an attorney."

This was getting stranger by the minute. I looked at Bobby. He could tell what I was thinking. We immediately headed for the door.

"Now just you wait a damn minute, you two sons of bitches," he yelled, jumping up out of his seat. "If you going where I think you going, you need to clear that with the Chief first. Ya hear me?" His voice trailed off as we headed out the door and toward the steps leading down to the first floor.

Something just didn't feel right. This was all wrapped up too neatly. There's no way she could have moved the body and it's unlikely she would have put the doll's dress on backward. Perhaps she was covering up for the real murderer?

CHAPTER FIVE

Leaving Pete alone with a suspect was risky. His idea of interrogation didn't exactly follow department guidelines. With that in mind, we proceeded to the first floor as quickly as we could, passing a noisy crowd of reporters who had somehow gained entry to City Hall. On the way down, we agreed I would handle the questioning while Bobby would observe from the surveillance window. I somehow failed to mention that I had never done this before. How hard could it be?

"Get these people outta here, *now*!" Bobby yelled to a dispatch officer as we passed the commotion in route to the interrogation room. Pete was closing the door behind him as we arrived.

"Well I'll be damned if it ain't the pride of Savannah. As usual, looks like you boys a day late and dollar short," he smirked, holding under his arm a folder—probably a signed confession. "Chief know ya'll down here?"

"Don't you worry about that" Bobby snapped, wisely stepping between the two of us.

"She's all yours," he said with a big wide grin as he turned and headed in the direction of the press waiting at the other end of the hall.

I entered the small dimly lit room while Bobby headed for the observation room next door. Once inside, I secured the latch, locking the door and slid a folding metal chair up to a small table in the center of the room. It was a rather odd arrangement with all walls including the ceiling painted black. A slow turning ceiling fan provided little relief from the stuffiness and strange odor in the room.

Sue Ellen was a petite woman, fortyish maybe, with long blonde hair. She seemed unaware of my presence as I sat down directly across from her.

"Smoke?" I asked. She looked down at the table without answering. "Mind if *I* smoke?"

She nodded slightly. I wasn't sure if that meant yes or no, so I lit up my last Marlboro.

"My name is Detective Monroe, Mrs. McKenna. I realize you've been through a lot this morning, but I have a few more questions I'd like to ask." She continued to look down without any acknowledgement or eye contact.

"I understand you've waived your right to an attorney so anything you say can be used as evidence against you. Did someone explain that to you?"

"Yeah," she answered finally, almost whispering but still looking down. "Why don't you just read the confession?"

"If you don't mind I'd like to hear it in your own words." She sat completely silent for what seemed like an eternity before finally speaking again.

"I killed him," she said quietly, voice shaking. "Isn't that what you people want to know?"

I remained silent hoping that would encourage her to continue, to no avail.

"Why?" I asked, finally breaking the long silence and dropping cigarette ashes directly on the table between us.

"Because he was a no good son of a bitch, that's why!" she answered, raising her voice for the first time. She rocked back and forth in her chair.

"In what way?"

She suddenly stopped rocking and finally raised her head. The dim overhead light exposed several large bruises under her right eye. She had a slightly deranged look on her face. It was strangely similar to the look on Willy Long's face a few years ago when he admitted to dismembering his wife while in my custody. I'll never forget that look.

"You married, Detective?" she asked, tracing an imaginary circle on the table with her index finger. "You're kinda cute."

I ignored the comment and leaned across the table as close as I could get to her.

"How'd you get those bruises on your face? Did your husband do that?" I asked.

She looked up at the ceiling fan smiling and began rocking in her chair again without answering. Back to square one.

"I need to know *exactly* what happened last night, Mrs. McKenna" I demanded, my voice rising and my frustration growing.

Again, we sat silently for a few moments before she unexpectedly exploded.

"Good Lord have mercy!" she yelled, slamming her fist on the table. "Goddammit! If I told that girl once, I told her a million times to stay away from that damn boy. You know that damn girl's got the devil in her don't you? That little tramp," she screamed.

Either she was clearly delusional or this was just an act. I wasn't sure which.

"Girl? What girl?"

She looked up at the ceiling again. Tears began to stream down both sides of her face.

"I killed that son of a bitch all right. Isn't that what you came here to hear me say?" Her voice suddenly dropped to a near silent whisper, while bowing her head as if she was about to pray.

Somehow, I just wasn't convinced. It just didn't add up, considering the evidence we had uncovered. In a strange way, I also felt sorry for her.

"Forgive me. I didn't mean to yell at you like that. I still don't understand what's going on. I thought jail is supposed to be a place for bad people," she said, wiping her eyes with her hand.

"It is" I replied, giving her a handkerchief.

"Well then, why am I here?" she asked, looking strangely confused. It was an odd question from someone who had just confessed to a murder.

I pulled my chair up and leaned forward as close to her as the table between us would allow. "You just signed a confession for the murder of your husband. You *are* aware of that aren't you? You could spend the rest of your life in a prison cell. Even worse, you could possibly get the death penalty. That's why you're here Ms. McKenna. You *do* understand that don't you?"

She nodded. For the first time she appeared to be somewhat remorseful. Perhaps reality had finally started to settle in.

"It's really important that you tell me what happened last night" I repeated, hoping to finally get a real answer. She took a deep breath and ran her fingers through her long blond hair before starting.

"Earl had been drinking a lot lately" she said slowly, looking down at the table between us.

"A lot?"

"Every night. That was unusual for him. He was a sociable drinker…a glass of wine now and then. As long as we'd been married I'd never known him to drink like that."

"Any idea why?" I asked, relieved she was finally starting to open up and talk. "When did that start?"

"I don't really know," she answered. "For the last few weeks he'd been coming home late almost every night. Whatever it was, I could tell it was getting to him. He just wasn't the same," she said wiping her eyes with the handkerchief I had given her. "He was… distant."

"Another woman perhaps?"

"Not likely" she said with a strange smirk.

"What about work. Did he ever talk about work? Was there something going on there?"

"He never discussed his work outside of the office. At least not with me."

I glanced at my watch expecting to be interrupted by the Chief any moment. "Let's get back to last night. I need you to tell me exactly what happened. She closed her eyes and tilted her head back as if she were staring at the ceiling.

"He was on the phone with Skeet" she began, rocking back and forth in her chair. "It was late."

"Skeet?" Who is that?" I asked.

"Mayor Wilson. Earl always called him Skeet. They grew up together right here in Savannah."

"How late was the call? Nine, ten, eleven?" I asked impatiently.

I'm not sure," she answered while reaching for my now empty pack of cigarettes on the table between us. "Midnight maybe. All I could hear was yelling and cursing."

"Where were you at that time?" I asked.

"Upstairs."

"Any idea what they might have been arguing about?" I asked as she started slowly rocking again, almost in a trance-like state.

"Something about Atlas" she finally answered, wiping her eyes again with the handkerchief. I made a quick entry in my notepad.

"The next thing I know, he was coming up the stairs cursing and shouting at me like *I'd* done something wrong. He was awful drunk."

"Why would he be angry at *you*?" She didn't answer.

"You said the two of you were upstairs. Upstairs where?"

"In my daughter's bedroom."

I glanced at my watch. There wasn't much time left before we'd need to get back upstairs.

"Continue."

"He came in yelling and screaming, blaming me. Telling me it was *my* fault."

"*Your* fault? *What* was your fault?" She didn't answer. Instead, she looked back down again at the table between us.

"I tried pushing him out of the way, but that's when he hit me."

"Is that how you got those bruises on your face? Did you fight back?" She looked up at the ceiling and began to smile.

"Do you really think I'd stand a chance against somebody his size?"

"So you struck him with a wooden doll? Is that what happened?"

"I don't remember," she answered slowly, looking down at the table again. "I don't remember anything but waking up and finding him lying on the floor."

"Was he still alive at that point?" I asked, trying to piece together the timeline.

"I don't know."

"Where was your husband's body when you left the house?"

"Still on the floor."

"In your daughter's bedroom?" She nodded.

"Where did you go after you left the house?"

"Tipper Lake," she answered. Bobby and I had passed there on our way up to the McKenna house this morning. It had to be at least a mile or two if not more from the house.

"Why Tipper Lake Mrs. McKenna?"

"We have a boat house there."

"Did anyone see you?"

"I don't know."

"And you stayed there all night?"

"Yes."

"So you set the house on fire before you left?" She seemed surprised by that question.

"No, but it was already burning when I got back the next morning." I glanced at the observation window to my left, surprised and wondering what Bobby was thinking.

"A house doesn't just go up in flames by itself. How do you think that happened?"

"Maybe it was just poetic justice," she said nonchalantly.

"How so?"

"If I didn't kill him, maybe the fire finished that son-of-a bitch. I hope he's burning in Hell right now!"

I could see the hatred in her eyes. It didn't appear to be a passing reaction either.

"Are we done yet Detective?" she asked, growing annoyed.

"Just a few more questions," I replied, quickly scribbling in my note pad. "Where was your daughter last night?"

She didn't answer. "Your daughter Ms. McKenna. Was she at home last night" I asked again.

"I don't know," she answered finally, looking down at the table again to avoid eye contact.

"You don't know?"

"I haven't seen my daughter in two years."

Before I could pursue that thread, we were interrupted by a knock at the door. I got up and unlocked it, opening it slightly.

"Wrap it up. We need to get the heck outta here," Bobby whispered through the cracked door. "I just got word that the Chief is on his way down here." As expected, that son of a bitch Andy had ratted us out.

I quietly closed the door and returned to the table. There was a lot more to this investigation than we had originally thought. There were several gaps in the timeline and inconsistencies in Sue Ellen McKenna's confession. I wasn't sure I completely believed everything I had just heard.

"Hopefully we'll get a chance to talk again soon Mrs. McKenna."

"So what happens now?" she asked looking confused.

"You just signed a full confession in the absence of legal counsel. It might be a little too late, but I'd advise you to get an attorney."

With her head lowered, she began to quietly sob as if the reality of what she had done had suddenly taken hold.

"Do you think I'm a *bad* person?" she asked with a frightened look on her face, wiping her eyes with the back of her hands.

Was it premeditated? Was it self-defense? I couldn't answer that question. I thanked her for her cooperation and headed for the door before turning around to ask one last question.

"Who is KJ?"

"KJ? I don't know who you're talking about" she answered.

"We found this upstairs outside your master bedroom."

I removed the medallion from my pocket and tossed it on the table in front of her. She picked it up and examined it for a second, then turned it over and read the inscription. Her eyebrows rose and she turned pale.

"I don't know any KJ," she answered, tossing the medallion back at me; it hit the floor. It was obvious she was lying.

"Are you sure you don't know who… "

"What the *hell* is going on down here?" yelled the chief, storming into the room, followed by the DA. "She's been questioned already. Didn't anyone tell you that we have a signed confession? I'm *surprised* at you Monroe," he yelled, pointing his finger in my face. "And you of all people know better than this," he fumed, turning to Bobby, standing behind him. "This isn't proper procedure. What the hell's gotten into the two of you?"

I stepped on the medallion lying on the floor. “Sorry Chief, we just had a hunch about something and I…”

“Hunch? Hunch my ass,” he yelled. “The only hunch you’ll be having is figuring out how long you and your partner will be escorting school children across the street.”

“Now hold on a minute Chief. This whole thing was my idea,” explained Bobby, stepping in front of me to create a distraction while I reached down to pick up the medallion.

“I don’t give a rat’s ass whose idea it was. We’ll talk about this later. Do I make myself clear?” he yelled, visibly angry.

I looked at Bobby without saying a word as we both made our way through the door, back through a narrow corridor and out the building’s side exit.

It was only two o’clock in the afternoon but it seemed much later. It had been one long morning and my guess is it would be an even longer afternoon and evening. We decided to grab a cup of coffee to discuss the strange trail of events we had just lived through.

CHAPTER SIX

The luncheonette at Long's Five & Dime was the best deal in town. The food wasn't great but the prices were cheap. Located in the center of town between Sears & Roebuck and the Greyhound bus terminal it remained open until nine. It was the perfect hangout for cops. Both Bobby and I were regulars for lunch and I probably had dinner there at least five times a week - today though, food wasn't on our minds. We needed to sort out the string of events that had taken place over the last twelve hours. We found a small side table in the back instead of our usual counter spot.

"I guess the Chief is pretty mad at us" Bobby said, nervously fumbling with the saltshaker.

"Yeah I know, but this whole thing seems pretty strange don't you think? For starters, a confession with no murder weapon? Really? And why not plead self-defense?"

"Yeah, I'm with you on that, and I don't understand why she came back to the scene of the crime," agreed Bobby. "And if she didn't start the fire, who did?"

"There are certainly holes in her story," I added looking around the diner mindful of others who might be in listening range. "It just doesn't add up."

"Maybe this will help" Bobby said, reaching into his coat pocket and taking out a several sheets of paper neatly folded and sliding it across the table in my direction.

"How in the hell did you get your hands on this?" I asked, taking a quick scan of the documents. It was a copy of Sue Ellen McKenna's signed confession.

"I got connections," he answered quietly while looking around the diner "but remember this case is basically closed. There's procedures and protocol that we're supposed to follow. We gotta be careful not to jeopardize this whole investigation. We're not above the law. You know that right?"

I didn't need a lecture about being above the law. I just had a feeling that something else was going on behind our backs and I didn't like it. This was all wrapped up and closed a little too neatly and a little too quickly.

"So you don't believe Sue Ellen's story?" he asked.

"Maybe some of it, but not all of it," I said, sliding the confession into my pocket, anxious to take a look, but aware that this was the wrong place and time to do it. "For starters, I don't believe she killed him. You and I know there's no way she could have dragged that body into the other room. Someone else had to do that."

"Right, but who?"

"The same person who put the dress on that doll backwards and tried to burn the evidence."

"So now what?" he asked, waiting for an answer.

"We should probably to pay a visit to the morgue to get a look at the body. It's possible we might find something there." For a few minutes we continued to plot our next steps, discussing the pros and cons before being interrupted by our favorite waitress.

"So what are you fine gentlemen having this afternoon?" she asked. "Today's special is a pulled pork sandwich with slaw and baked beans. All for just $2."

"Just coffee, thanks."

"Speak for yourself Youngblood," answered Bobby, adjusting his hearing aid. "Pulled pork huh? Man, that *does* sound mighty good, but I think I'll just have me a piece of that pecan pie. Could ya put a little whipped cream on top and bring me a tall sweet tea – no ice, no lemon." He removed two of his diabetes pills and placed them on a napkin next to the saltshaker.

"One coffee, one sweet tea and a slice of pecan pie coming right up. By the way, nice shoes Detective," she added with a wink and a smile directed at me before turning away.

Danita was the afternoon waitress at the diner. She was a young tall attractive colored lady with a pretty brown complexion and long dark brown hair pulled back into a ponytail. She wore a white apron tied tight at the waist over her navy blue uniform. She had a great personality and always gave us extra special attention whenever we came in. Despite the protests and luncheonette sit-ins across the South, Long's still refused to serve Negroes at the counter, but had no reservations about them working *behind* the counter. Segregation was still alive and well in Savannah.

"You know I think that girl's got a thing for you, boy."

"Whatever."

"You trying to tell me you don't notice the way she smiles at you every time we come in here?"

"Look, she's a waitress. It's her *job* to smile."

"She never smiles at *me* like that. If I was a good lookin' fella like you wearing them fancy clothes and hipster shoes, I might have a chance. If you ask me, I think she wants a little *milk in her coffee*...know what I mean?" he chuckled. I ignored the comment although we *had* secretly gone out a few times. Right now the subject of women was the last thing on my mind. I removed the medallion from my pocket and examined the engraving again, flipping it from side to side.

"I think Sue Ellen knows who this belongs to. You saw her reaction when I showed it to her. She also mentioned something about not having seen her daughter in two years? What's the story behind that?"

Instead of answering the question, he looked down at the table and began nervously fumbling with the saltshaker. He appeared flustered and remained silent for a moment before taking off his glasses and carefully placing them on the table.

"Being as though you're new around here, you don't know the full story," he began slowly in low voice. "A couple of years ago Sue Ellen and Earl reported their daughter, Catherine, missing.

She was sixteen at the time. The whole thing had to do with an argument over some boy at school she was messing around with... typical teenage stuff. That led to a bigger fight at home. Next day, she runs away. Nobody seemed too concerned, so we didn't make any real effort to follow up on it. You know how kids are. They say they're running away from home and then they show up the next day. Well, a week passed with no word from or sign of Catherine so we broadened the search throughout the entire county but came up empty handed. No clues. Nothing. Today, she's still missing."

"One black coffee, nice and hot, and a pecan pie," said Danita with a big wide grin, setting our order on the table in front of us. "I'll be right back with your sweet tea sir. Will there be anything else gentlemen?"

"Thanks, I think we're all set," I answered, avoiding eye contact and waiting for her to leave before picking up where we left off.

"So the case is still open?"

"Yeah."

"I've got a pretty good idea who dropped the ball on this one."

"No," he answered, still looking down. His body language and facial expression mirrored regret. "It was *my* case."

That was an unexpected bombshell, completely out of character for him. In the short time we had worked together I had gained a great deal of respect for his thoroughness.

"I probably coulda done more, but I didn't. I just screwed up on that one." He scratched his head and paused for a moment before putting his glasses back on and adjusting his hearing aid.

"I've been on this job for a long time and I've dealt with a lot difficult things, but this one haunts me every single day." He paused again before continuing. "Losing a child is the greatest pain you can ever experience as a parent. I've been there. I know what they're going through. I can't tell you how many times I've prayed to the good Lord Almighty for closure. I got six months left and if this case is connected in any way with her disappearance, then solving it would finally put my mind at ease. I feel like I owe Sue Ellen and Earl that much, if not more. The Bible says, *"For I know my transgressions, and my sin is ever before me."*

I opened a new pack of Marlboros, lit a smoke and took a long drag before exhaling. I had more than enough on my plate already. Taking this on could complicate the commitments I had made with the Feds, but I could tell this would really mean a lot to him. He needed closure and deserved an opportunity to finish his career with respect and peace of mind. Who knows? Perhaps there *was* some strange connection between the two. On the other hand, both the Chief and the DA were determined to close this case as soon as possible. Getting more involved than we already were could be risky.

"You realize we could be jeopardizing our jobs by doing this don't you?"

"I got six months before retiring. I ain't got nothing to lose," Bobby answered.

That was a statement I couldn't make, but I reached over—somewhat reluctantly—and gave him a firm handshake.

"Okay, so what's your plan?"

CHAPTER SEVEN

"For the love of Christ man don't you *ever* stop smoking? Breathing that stuff makes me sick!" Bobby grumbled.

I took one last drag before pinching the end and placing it behind my ear for later.

"Happy now?"

He kept his eyes fixed on the road without answering and signaled a left turn by extending his arm through the window. We turned onto a dirt road and traveled another half mile before stopping at the edge of a gravel driveway. A large Rottweiler chained to a wooden fence barked loudly as we pulled up behind an old Studebaker station wagon.

"Hush!" he yelled before shutting off the engine and applying the parking break, putting his full weight on it in order to get it to remain engaged. He got out and headed up the driveway towards a small trailer as I slammed the passenger side door repeatedly in order to get it to close. We had Pete and Andy's old squad car today while repairs were being made to our car. Our wreck had stalled out three times his week, causing me to miss the Chief's morning briefings. Not that this one was any better.

The Rottweiler charged down the driveway as far as his chain would allow, then stopped and waited patiently as we approached. Bobby crouched down on one knee and gave him a big hug. "This here's my number one buddy, old Tracker."

"That's one big ass dog," I said, keeping my distance.

"Naw, he's just a pup. He ain't even finished growing yet. By this time next year he'll be twice this size." He adjusted the red handkerchief around the dog's neck and uncoupled the chain to turn him loose. Once loose, he ran over to the trailer's steps, stopping in front of an empty feeding bowl.

"It's just been the two of us for last five years," he said, standing up and brushing the dog hair from his shirt. "I couldn't ask for a better friend."

I envied him. I'd always dreamed of having a dog as a kid but moving constantly from city to city had made that impractical. Too bad – they made for great companions and, unlike most people, were always there for you.

"Speaking of dogs, you know you need to train that dog a' yours, boy. It don't make no sense, you letting that dog pee all over the place. That's just nasty…*and* lazy. You can catch a disease or something. Just take him for a walk in the morning before you leave for work," he suggested, walking over to a large wooden barrel with a metal top. "Heck, I *might even catch something* just going over there." He reached into the barrel to pull out a handful of dog food.

"Nice little place you got here," I said, ignoring him. Since coming to Savannah, I had "adopted" a stray dog I'd found sleeping in an abandoned car during one of my investigations. It was the closest thing I'd ever had to a real pet.

After filling up the dog's bowl he headed up the steps and into the small singlewide trailer. I followed behind.

"Excuse the mess. Go ahead and make yourself at home." I looked for a place to sit as he turned on a small rotating fan and opened a window, holding it in place with a long wooden stick. I hoped that would help cool down the stifling heat inside the trailer, a sparsely furnished large open room with a wood stove in the center. It was clear from the smell that his dog spent a considerable amount of time inside as well as outside. To my left was an old rocking chair facing a small television, and to my right, an old white refrigerator on top of a small wooden pallet. Above the refrigerator hung a picture of his retirement dream – the 57' Chris Craft Constellation with the twin Chrysler V8 engines. Framed photographs of all sizes and shapes covered just about every square inch of the other two walls. One in particular had a large wooden frame surrounded by four small silver crosses.

"Is this Erleen?" I asked, staring at a picture of a much younger Bobby, perhaps early twenties, standing next to an attractive young lady. He walked over to the picture and studied it for a moment before carefully wiping the dust off the glass with his hand.

"Yeah, that's my sweetheart, the love of my life," he replied proudly, staring at the picture. She had long blonde hair and the prettiest smile I'd ever seen.

"Met her down at the courthouse where she was working in the mailroom. Man, if she wasn't the *prettiest* thing I'd ever seen. I used to make up excuses to go down to the courthouse everyday just to see her. I bet I spent more time down there than I did in the office," he said smiling. He was right. She *was* a beautiful woman.

"They say time heals all wounds…you learn to live with the pain." He shook his head. "Well, I'm still trying," he said sadly. "The honest truth is you *never* get over it. The pain stays with you forever. But that's life ain't it?" We both stood there silently staring at the picture.

"You ever lose someone close to you?" he asked, still looking at the picture. I remained silent.

"See that boat right there?" he asked, pointing to a small boat in the picture behind the two of them. "I proposed to her on that boat. I gave old Bud Tompkins five dollars to let me rent it for a couple of hours and took her way, way out on Tipper Lake. Man, that old thing barely made it out there. I wasn't so sure we'd make it back either," he chuckled. "I did it right there."

"Well, what did she say?" I asked. His face lit up with a big smile.

"What you think she said boy? I told her either she said yes or she was gonna swim back to shore," he laughed, stomping his foot on the floor. It was the first time I had heard him laugh since we'd become partners. He fell silent, staring at the picture for a moment before looking away and exhaling, his smile disappearing just as quickly as it had appeared.

"Go ahead and rest ya legs and make yourself at home," he suggested, finally breaking the awkward silence. "I'll just be a minute." He disappeared into a back room while I opened a metal folding chair and placed it near a small wooden table with a stack of bibles and several sheets of paper in the center. At the edge of the table was a small ashtray with a half-smoked cigar - Red Label, probably Cuban. That was odd, considering his dislike of smoking. Being nosy, I peeked at one of the sheets in the center. On it was a bunch of scribbled notes.

> *Blessed are they that mourn: for they shall be comforted. Matthew 5:4*
>
> *For though I be absent in the flesh, yet am I with you in the spirit, joying and beholding your order and the steadfastness of your faith in Christ. Colossians 2:5*
>
> *And ye now therefore have sorrow: but I will see you again, and your heart shall rejoice, and your joy no man....*

I quickly placed the sheet of paper back on the table as the door opened. He reemerged carrying a brown leather briefcase under his arm. He placed it on the floor next to the front door.

"Is that a Cuban? Can you buy those around here?"

He walked over to the small refrigerator without answering, removed a bottle of soda, and popped the cap with his pocketknife.

I used that opportunity to place the sheets back in order while his back was turned.

"How long were you and Erleen married?" I asked, curious to know more about the love of his life.

"Thirty-seven glorious years," he answered, pulling up a chair across from me and sitting down. He tossed the cap in a wastebasket nearby. "A car accident took her life on her way to work. I was supposed to drive her to work that day, but I was too lazy. I let her take the car instead." He took a long sip and wiped his mouth with the back of his hand then placed the bottle on the table between us. "For years I blamed myself for what happened, but now I know it was just God's will."

"You really believe that?"

"Yeah I do," he confirmed, staring at the picture on the wall. "It's not our place to question God's actions. Proverbs says, *"Trust in the LORD with all thine heart; and lean not unto thine own understanding."*

Here we go again, I thought.

"When she died, a part of me also died that day," he said sadly. "I didn't know how to deal with the guilt." He removed his pistol from the holster on his hip. "I was so miserable one day that I actually filled this chamber and placed the barrel in my mouth. Can you believe that? I was a mess. But that would have been too easy. I wanted to know *why* she was taken away from me. I tried just about everything…counseling, support groups, you name it. Nothing worked. In time I found peace in the church, but I was still angry. It just wasn't fair, but it was God's plan. At the time I just didn't understand that. It didn't make any sense to me. I wasn't raised in the church so to me, God wasn't real, know what I mean? I've felt that way all my life. Just before she passed however, I remember her saying that there comes a time in everyone's life when they have to decide *whether or not they believe.* We can live with the pain for the rest of our lives or we can put our faith in a higher power to explain our loss. Sooner or later, *we all have to make that decision,"* he said, looking at me directly.

Rather than start an argument, I remained silent.

"I reckon I'm preaching to the wall" he said, smiling before reaching across the table and placing his hand on mine.

"You remember the time you told me about that situation you had up north."

"Situation?"

"You know, about that lady you were engaged to …the one that caught you out in the street with her sister. As I recollect, she pointed a gun at your head. Your gun, I might add. And…" he paused, waiting for me the finish the story.

"…and pulled the trigger," I said, reluctantly.

"But it jammed," he said, with a big wide grin on his face.

"And your point is?" I asked, making a mental note never to tell anyone that story again.

"From your point of view I suppose you'd call that a fluke that you didn't get your stupid head blown off that day. Did you ever think that maybe, just maybe it was the grace of God that kept you from lying in a pool of your own blood that day?"

"I guess I just got lucky," I snapped back.

"No," he said, shaking his head. "Luck ain't got anything to do with it. The grace of God spared your life that day. For all intents and purposes you should be buried in a wooden box right now, but you ain't. It just wasn't yo' time. The Almighty obviously has a purpose for your life. He ain't finished with you yet. Either you just don't realize that, or you just too hard headed to admit it."

Maybe he had a point. Could it be God had decided that day, that a more fitting punishment for cheating would be to live and work in Savannah? If so, I think I would have preferred the bullet.

"You can't live in denial forever. Believe me, I tried, but the minute I chose to believe in God's power, it felt like a large weight had been lifted off my shoulders. Now you can continue to believe in *luck* and *coincidence*, but one day *you will witness the presence of the Almighty*. At some point in our lives we all will. It's just a matter of time. You might deny it when it happens, *but you will experience His Presence*. I guarantee it."

"You *really* believe that don't you?"

"As God is my witness, I know it to be true," he replied.

"Can we save this for another time? It's getting late and we need to get over to the morgue to examine the body," I suggested, eager to end this conversation.

He turned off the fan, closed the window and locked the front door on our way out, stopping for a second to pet his dog. He placed the brown leather briefcase in the trunk, never saying a word about it or what it contained.

CHAPTER EIGHT

This would be the third time this week I'd miss the Chief's afternoon briefing to take care of some personal business, but I couldn't miss my appointment at Willow Manor. Three weeks had passed since my last visit and I was anxious to get an update.

I locked the apartment door, exited the building and quickly marched up the street in search of the nearest phone booth. If I recall, there was one a few blocks away. I entered the booth, looked both ways and gave the phone a good hard wallop on top to get a dial tone. Never fails. It was an old trick I'd learned as a kid. I took a quick look at my watch before dialing.

"Savannah PD, Detective Thomas speaking. How can I help you?" answered the voice on the other end of the line.

"It's me."

"Where you been? Chief's been looking for you."

"I've got some business to take care of this afternoon. Can you cover for me?" I asked. The line went silent.

"All right, I'll cover for ya" he answered finally, "but you can't keep doing this. Understand?"

"Thanks."

"By the way, you all set for tonight?" he asked.

"Yeah. I'm good."

"You sure?"

"I said yeah, all right?" I hung up the phone, ending the discussion. As I walked over to the squad car parked at the end of the street I noticed a young boy on both knees in front of an old column front two-story home. His arm appeared to be stuck in a small opening between the front steps leading up to the porch.

"What's the matter kid?" He looked up for a second without answering. The look on his face was one of frustration. "Your arm stuck?"

He carefully removed his arm from the opening, got up, and brushed a patch of dirt from his blue jeans. He was no more than seven or eight years old. On the right side of his face was a bandage surrounded by several dark bruises. He appeared worried.

"My baseball's under the porch," he answered frantically. "Can you help me get it? I done already lost one and my nana's gonna kill me if I lose another one." I glanced at my watch. I was already late, what the hell. A few more minutes wouldn't make any difference.

"Show me where it's at."

He stooped down and pointed to the narrow opening behind the wooden stairs leading up to the front porch. I took off my jacket, folded it neatly and placed it on one of the steps.

"You a policeman?" he asked, staring at the holster under my arm now in full view.

"Something like that," I answered, stooping down to get a better look through the small gap between the steps and porch.

"I bet you shoot bad guys just like Dick Tracy don't you?" he asked making an imaginary gun with his index finger and pointing it at me. I moved to the other side of the steps to get a look from a different angle. From that side I could clearly see the ball through the gap. It was too far to reach by hand but if I could find something long enough to reach it perhaps I could force it to roll in this direction. A quick look around the yard turned up a dead branch from a nearby tree. That might do the trick. It certainly looked long enough. I got it and slowly inserted it between the gap and maneuvered the ball in my direction, close enough to grab it.

"Try being a little more careful next time kid," I suggested, tossing it to him.

"Gee thanks Mister!" He stuffed the ball in his pocket and pulled a baseball cap over his neatly cut blonde hair.

"What happened to your face" I asked, slinging my jacket over one shoulder.

"I fell." A fall doesn't make bruises like those. Judging from their location, it was pretty obvious what where they came from.

"Where's your folks kid?" I asked.

"I live with my nana," he answered, looking away.

"What about your mom and dad?"

"My daddy's in the army. Nana says the war gonna be over soon and he'll be coming home," he said quietly, sitting down on one of the steps. "He sends me letters every month. Nana reads them to me. When he comes home we're gonna go to the picture show, play baseball and have lots of fun," he said, his face suddenly lighting up with big smile. "Do you know when the war is gonna be over Mister?" I assuming the "war" was Vietnam and I'm sure no one knew when it would end. It was a pointless war that we had no business being involved in. It could go on for years.

"I'm afraid I don't but while your daddy's gone, you're the man of the house. That means taking care of your nana and doing what she tells you to do. Understand young man?" He nodded, yes. I took out a piece of gum, split it in two and gave him half. Then I sat down on the step beside him.

"I wanna be a army man just like my daddy and shoot bad guys too," he said, making a pistol with his thumb and forefinger. That comment brought a smile to my face.

"I once knew a kid just like you. His daddy wasn't home much either because he had an important job to do, just like your daddy."

"Was he a army man too?"

"No he wasn't, but what he did helped a lot of people just like your daddy."

"Did he see his daddy a lot?" the kid asked.

"No…no, he didn't."

"Did that make him sad?" he asked.

"A lot," I answered after reflecting for moment. "Unlike the other kids' daddies, his dad never had the time to do any fun stuff with him, like playing baseball or going to the movies."

"So what happened to that kid?" he asked curiously.

"He was a skinny kid that the bullies at school always picked on. As a matter of fact, he would come home with bruises on his face just like yours. His daddy was always too busy to spend time with him and never taught him how to take care of himself. One day the kid decided he couldn't take it anymore so he dropped out of school."

"Did his folks know?" the kid asked.

"No. He got up every day as if he was going to school but instead would spend the whole day hanging out on the streets. One day he got caught stealing from a grocery store."

"Did he go to jail?" he asked.

"Luckily he was too young" I answered, "but the policeman who caught him made a deal with him. If the kid agreed to go back to school, he wouldn't tell his parents about the grocery store. I think you and I know what would have happened if his parents had found out right?"

"A whuppin," he answered squirming nervously on the step.

"You got that right," I said. "Also as a part of the deal, the kid would have to come down to the police station after school every day, where they'd meet in the gym so the kid could learn how to box and defend himself. For the first time in his life, the kid had a friend and a safe place he could call home.

"So the officer was like a daddy to him?" he asked. I thought about that for a moment. It had never occurred to me.

"I guess you could say that. As a matter of fact, the kid decided that one day he too would be a policeman and help others as the police at his police station had helped him."

"That's a good story." "What happened to the kid?" he asked.

"He grew up and became a police officer. Eventually he was promoted to a Detective."

"What about the officer who helped the kid?" he asked.

"Noah. Who you talking to boy?" yelled a voice from inside the house.

"A policeman, Nana, and he got a gun under his coat like Dick Tracy. He shoots bad guys too just like Poppa," he answered. "Come see!"

"Now you just stop making up stories you hear, Boy" said a woman pushing open the screen door and stepping onto the front porch. "You need to get in here and finish…"

"I'm awful sorry Ma'am for keeping the boy from his chores," I interrupted, "but I just happened to be walking by and he seemed awful upset about his ball."

"That's the third ball I've bought you this month boy. You must think money grows on trees," she said with both hands on her hips, looking directly at him and not at me.

"I didn't lose it Nana, see?" he answered, holding it up for her to see.

"Well thank the Lord," she said, "and to you as well Sir," finally turning to me. She was an older woman with long red hair and patches of grey pulled back into a ponytail held with a flowered scarf tied around her head. She wore a light cotton blue dress with a white apron tied loosely at her waist.

"JoAnn Reynolds," she said, stepping to the edge of the porch and extending her hand. "Looks like you've already met Noah," she added.

"Yeah. Good kid. We've been talking about his dad. Nam, I presume?"

"Three long years this November. When will this stupid war end?" she asked. "Why is this country always getting in to something that ain't none of their business anyway?" she asked. "Don't make no sense to me."

"Ma'am I don't…"

"Don't get me started," she snapped, throwing her hands in the air while turning around to go back inside.

"Noah. The kitchen floor and the mop are still waiting for you," she reminded, voice trailing off as she disappeared into the house with the screen door slamming behind her.

"You heard Nana," said the kid. He held out his hand. "Thanks for getting my baseball. Can you come back sometime and tell me more stories?" he asked.

"Sure. Maybe I'll even throw in a few boxing lessons. How about that?"

"Really?" he answered, eyes lighting up

"Really!" I yelled as he hurried up the steps and disappeared inside the house. I glanced at my watch. I'd lost track of time, but it was well worth the stroll down memory lane.

CHAPTER NINE

"Excuse me sir. Can I be of assistance?" asked a young lady at the front desk.

"Yes. I'm here to see Ms. Albright."

"Would you mind having a seat across the hall? Someone should be with you shortly to take you up to her room."

I took a seat across the hall as I was told, along with several other visitors waiting to see their loved ones as well. The waiting room was meticulously furnished with mahogany furniture throughout. Textured wallpaper covered every wall and beautiful flower arrangements decorated each table. Directly across from a massive bay window stood an antique fireplace with a solid brass mantle. It was quite elegant for a place like this.

"Mr. Monroe?"

I raised my hand and stood up.

"Would you mind following me sir?" asked a cute young nurse dressed in a white uniform and a light blue jacket. I nodded and proceeded behind her to the end of a long hall and up a set of wooden stairs.

"Is this your first time here at Willow Manor?"

"Yes, as a matter of fact it is."

"Well let me tell you a little about our facility," she offered as we walked down a long corridor, careful to avoid a young Negro boy mopping up a spill in the corner.

"Willow Manor is one of the most prestigious convalescent homes for long term care in the state of Georgia. We were established over thirty years ago with a generous gift from the Thomas C. Willow family. You are familiar with the Willow family, aren't you?"

"Of course." I had absolutely no idea who she was talking about.

"Since our beginning, we've cared for the family members of two senators, three governors, and one former president. This building we're currently in is actually a part of the original Willow estate. On the other side of the parking lot is our new expansion added about five years ago. It's increased our number of beds to over a hundred."

"I'm impressed. It's a beautiful facility."

"Well, thank you. We do our best to serve the needs of your loved ones. Rest assured, you're mother is in good hands."

We continued down the hall, stopping at Room 378, where she used her pen to enter something on a clipboard attached to the room's door, before opening the door and standing aside.

"Dr. Samuelson will be here in a minute to speak with you. In the meantime there's a nurse's station at the end of the hall," she added, pointing to her left. "If you need anything just ask for me."

"Thanks Natalie," I said, reading from the nametag pinned to her blouse. I watched as she turned and headed away. Nice legs.

Compared to the fancy lobby and waiting room, it was a very simple, no frills room. Although the windows were fully open, it still had that antiseptic hospital smell. A single bed faced a large picture window overlooking the courtyard. Next to the bed was a small nightstand, the top covered with framed pictures - reminders of memories I would rather forget.

She sat motionless, facing the window with pillows supporting her back and head. Covering her face was a breathing device with several tubes attached to a small tank behind the bed. I quietly pulled a chair next to the bed and sat down, not sure if she was aware of my presence or not. I had avoided this day for months, but overcome by a feeling of guilt, I knew sooner or later this day would come. Considering the circumstances, I didn't know where to start.

"Mr. Monroe?" asked a short gentleman wearing a long white coat, entering the room. He wore a pair of black thick-lensed glasses and sported a bright red tie. He had a terrible comb-over, which covered his receding hairline.

I stood up and moved the chair back against the wall.

"Yeah?"

"Mark Samuelson, Ms. Albright's personal caretaker," he replied, extending his hand and holding a clipboard under his other arm.

"You mean, her doctor?"

"Here at Willow Manor, we prefer to be identified as *personal caretakers,*" he answered, shaking my hand.

"How's she doing?"

"The stroke has damaged part of her brain. She's paralyzed and unable to speak or move, but there does appear to be some brain activity. That means she does hear and can understand what we're saying. It's a very unusual condition. While there is some research being done in Boston regarding this type of condition, the extent of the damage unfortunately would rule out any significant recovery."

This wasn't great news, but perhaps there was still *some* hope.

"I'd be glad to go over her charts with you," he offered, removing the clipboard from under his arm.

"Thanks and I appreciate all you've done so far—but if you don't mind I'd rather have some time alone with her."

"By all means Mr. Monroe. Don't hesitate to contact me at any time if you have any questions or concerns."

"Thanks Doc."

He headed towards the door, turning around before leaving. "Also, would you mind stopping by the billing office on your way out? There's a…" here he paused for an uncomfortable moment, "matter of several outstanding invoices that require your immediate attention."

"Of course Doctor." Money had been a little tight lately. I was still maintaining a place in New York for the past six months under the expectation of returning soon. Hopefully I could work out something with this facility.

I sat back down next to the bed as he closed the door behind him. At seventy-five, she was still a beautiful woman. Her long auburn hair, streaked with grey, had been combed and styled just the way she liked. She looked peaceful. Still, it was emotionally hard to see someone I loved so much in this condition.

I sat quietly for a few minutes, confused and not really sure how to say what I was feeling. It's the simple things that are hardest to say. Finally, I pulled myself together, wiped my eyes and leaned over close to her.

"It's been a rough year, but…I'm doing okay now," I whispered. "I got a job down here. It's not the greatest job in the world, but it'll do for now and it got me closer to you. I'll never forget all the things you've done for me… all the sacrifices, all the…" I paused for moment, struggling with conflicting emotions. In my line of work it was necessary to built a tough, unemotional exterior. I had become insensitive to pain, or so I thought. At this moment however I felt a deep sense of hopelessness. It was a feeling I'd never experienced at any point in my life before.

I closed my eyes and held her hand next to my face, before taking a deep breath and starting again.

"I finally got the courage to speak to my father. I really tried in my heart to forgive him for what he did, but I can't. I know that's wrong, but that's the way I feel. Please try to understand. Maybe one day that'll change, I don't know."

I sat there for a few moments in silence before removing a small book from my pocket. I found the marker and pressed back the pages just as Natalie entered. I quickly and discreetly wiped the tears that had collected in both eyes.

"Excuse me for interrupting Mr. Monroe, but it's time for Ms. Albright's medication. I'm very sorry. Would you mind waiting outside? It'll only take a minute or two."

"No problem. I was…just about to leave anyway, but I'd really appreciate it if you could do me a big favor."

"Certainly Mr. Monroe. We're here to serve her every need."

"Would you mind reading a few pages from this book to Ms. Albright each day?" I handed her a worn, paperback copy of *The Complete Poems of Emily Dickinson*. "It would really mean a lot to me."

"Certainly" she answered, taking a look at the cover before placing it on the nightstand. "Emily Dickinson… great choice. I'll make it a point to read to her every day."

I placed the chair back in the corner of the room and tied the curtains back so she could see the beautiful scenery outside. I placed her arms back under the cover and whispered in her ear that I loved her more than anything in this world. It was the first time in my life I'd ever told anyone that. As I closed the door behind me, I took one last look. Call me crazy, but for a second, it almost appeared as if she actually smiled at me.

An overturned trailer combined with a heavy downpour, slowed traffic to a crawl on the interstate heading back toward Savannah.

In between the stop and start slowdowns, I thought about how unfair life truly was. How could such a wonderful God-fearing person deserve this fate, while worthless, no good criminals continued to roam the streets committing vicious crimes? Bobby had said that things happen for a reason. It was God's plan. *What a bullshit excuse!* If there really was a God, then he certainly had a perverted sense of right and wrong.

CHAPTER TEN

By the time I got back to Savannah the rain had become more of a light drizzle. Trying to dodge potholes full of water felt more like driving on an obstacle course than a city street. I took a right on Columbus and a quick left at the Texaco station to avoid going through the center of town at this hour. A familiar figure walked quickly down the street about a block from the intersection, holding a newspaper over her head and carefully sidestepping the deep puddles left behind. I slowed down, pulled over, and rolled down my window.

"It's awfully late to be walking in this part of town alone don't you think?" The figure stopped and cautiously stared at me through the window opening for a moment before answering.

"Now ain't *you* a sight for sore eyes," answered a surprised Danita.

"What are *you* doing out this time of night?" I asked.

"The evening shift girl didn't show up so they asked me to do a double. We were real busy this evening and I missed my bus to get home so I decided to walk. So what's your story?" she asked.

"You shouldn't be walking through this part of town," I answered, avoiding her question.

"It don't bother me. Besides, I could use the money," she replied. "Gotta do what you gotta do. Know what I mean?"

By now it was getting late and I still had another stop to make, but I decided that could wait. I tossed my jacket in the back seat and unlocked the passenger door.

"I'll take you home. Get in."

"You sure you want to drop me off in *my* part of town at this hour?" she asked getting in and slamming the door shut, before using a handkerchief to wipe the rain from the side of her face.

It didn't faze me. Couldn't be any worse than Harlem or Bed-Sty late at night.

"Why should I be worried? You should be more concerned about what your neighbors are gonna think when they see you coming home in a police car."

I put the car back in gear and gave it a little gas just as Bobby had suggested, careful not to flood the engine. A large sign posted on the opposite side of the street caught my attention as we pulled off. It was posted in front of a construction site - Atlas Construction Company. The name was familiar, but I couldn't recall where I'd heard it before.

"Maybe they'll think I finally cut that no-good man of mine who ignores me."

"Give me a break. I've been busy."

"Busy, or a new woman?" she snapped, tossing her wet newspaper out the window.

Women.

By the time we got to Park Hill the rain had stopped and the humidity had returned with a vengeance. People were sitting outside on steps covered with newspaper and children were playing in the rain soaked streets. Like most major cities in the South, segregation divided the city down the middle - colored people on one side, and whites on the other. Both sides were self-contained communities with their own schools, stores and businesses. It reminded me of several parts of Harlem and the Bronx. We eventually stopped at a small white one level house with an unfinished driveway and a grassy lot that badly needed attention.

"I'll wait here until you get inside," I suggested, removing a half finished cigarette from the ashtray and searching my pockets for a match.

She got out and walked up a muddy unpaved driveway, stopping at the front door. A bright orange envelope had been wedged between the doorknob and the doorframe – most likely an eviction notice. She glanced at the contents briefly before ripping the envelope in half and tossing it on the ground. Visibly upset, she headed back down the driveway. What could be worse than working all day and coming home to find out you've been locked out? I could relate having been in that situation before in New York. Fortunately unlike New York, they don't dump all of your belongings out on the street.

"That son of a bitch locked me out. I told him I'd have his damn money by the end of the week. That's *tomorrow*. He couldn't wait *just one more day*?"

From what I could see, the only thing keeping her from entering was a cheap padlock around the doorknob. I checked my watch and, against my better judgment, shut off the engine. I cautiously trekked up the muddy driveway, mindful of messing up my good shoes. She followed close behind. I could see neighbors peeping through the blinds next door.

"Official police business. You'd better stand back Miss," I said loud enough for the neighbors to hear. I gave Danita a wink just before kicking the door in. I drew my weapon making sure the neighbors were still watching and stepped inside the small, sparsely furnished home. Although it was dark inside I was able to find a light switch next to the door. The power had been shut off. I placed my weapon back in its holster.

"It's safe to come in" I yelled, "but it looks like your power's been shut off."

She walked in slowly, feeling her way around in what appeared to be the living room. I closed the door behind her and followed her into the dark room.

"You can't stay here tonight. Do you have another place to stay? I asked." She gave me a long stare before answering.

"Don't worry about me. I'll be fine," she said sarcastically.

"What's your problem?" I asked, confused at her sudden change in attitude.

"You know *damn well* what my problem is Mr. high and mighty Detective" she snapped, pointing her finger in my face. "You come to the luncheonette damn near every day and ignore me like I don't even exist and then beg me to come over to your place to spend the night."

"If it's an apology you want, then…I'm sorry okay? You need to remember where we are. I can't just parade around town with you. You know that. I've got a job and a career to worry about. And what was I supposed to do the other day? I couldn't let my partner in and you were still asleep."

"So it's just a sex thing. That what it's all about ain't it, or am I *just another one of your friends*?"

"You're not *listening* to me woman."

"Oh I'm *listening*, and don't give me that 'I got a job to worry about' crap. I wasn't born yesterday. And why should you even care? They don't like you *anyway*" she said.

"Who?"

"Them other two detectives. I hear them talking about you all the time at lunch."

"You mean Pete and Andy?"

"Yeah, those two assholes that never leave a tip."

"What are they saying?"

"They don't trust you. They don't understand why someone like you would leave New York City for a place like this. To tell the truth, I'm not so sure I understand that either" she said. She fell silent, waiting for a response. I kept silent, instead staring down at the floor. Maybe one day I could tell her. I just couldn't afford to take that risk right now.

Frustrated, she sat down on a small red sofa near the door. It had been a very long day and we were both tired. I certainly wasn't in the mood for a fight and I knew she felt the same way. I picked up a pillow next to her, tossed it on the floor and sat down beside her, still not sure what to say.

"I guess we're not going to settle this tonight," she finally relented, after realizing an explanation wasn't forthcoming. "But at some point we *do* need to talk about it. You promise?" she asked, raising an eyebrow. I wasn't really sure if I agreed but nodded anyway.

"Yeah. I promise. We'll talk," I answered, hoping she'd be satisfied for the moment.

She flashed a slight grin before giving me a kiss. I let out a quiet sigh of relief.

With that out of the way for the moment, we needed to focus on what to do about tonight.

"Grab some clothes. You can stay with me tonight" I decided, somewhat reluctantly. "Make sure you also grab anything that might be valuable." She disappeared into a back room before returning a few minutes later with a large suitcase.

The Feds had been hounding me for an update and I'd gotten distracted with the McKenna case. Hopefully I could hold them off a little while longer until I had something more substantial to report. Adding a new houseguest into the mix could also complicate things even more.

CHAPTER ELEVEN

"What time is it?"

"Seven o'clock," she answered, sitting on the edge of the bed with a plastic bag over the curlers in her hair underneath.

"Seven o'clock? Why is the TV on at 7 o'clock in the morning?" I mumbled while putting a pillow over my head to get back to sleep.

"Hush. I'm listening to the news. Don't you wanna know what's going on?" she answered, pounding on the pillow just to irritate me. She got out of bed to adjust the coat-hanger antenna wrapped with aluminum foil to get better television reception.

"Did the Yankees win?" I asked.

"Is that all you care about?" she answered, pounding the pillow again.

"President Kennedy's on the news talking 'bout putting a man on the moon before the end of the 60's. Why go spending all that money for nothing? I mean, really…what they expect to find up there anyway?"

I removed the pillow and turned over, somewhat surprised to hear that. "What about the missiles in Cuba?"

"The missiles? What planet you been on? That's old news, Baby. The Russians backed off. Didn't you know that? The big news this morning is all about that woman killing her husband. Probably caught him messing around with some other woman. What's the matter with you men anyway? I woulda killed that fool too, but I don't know why she had to burn up that house, though. That was a real nice house." I sat up, pulled back the cover and wiped my eyes.

"What do *you* know about that house?"

"My neighbor did some handy work for them. He used to talk my ear off all the time about how nice that house was. Nice wood floors, big spiral staircase in the…"

"Your neighbor? What neighbor?"

"Mr. Lester, my next door neighbor. You know, the one peeping through the blinds last night when we drove up."

"Handy work, huh?"

"Yeah. Him and Sonny Boy."

"Sonny Boy? Who's Sonny Boy?" I asked. She looked at me as if I were an idiot.

"His *son,*" she said, emphasizing *son*. "Every now and then he'd take Sonny with him to help out."

"Did he ever say anything about the people who lived there?"

"He worked for the woman. I guess her husband was never there. He always talked about how nice she was to him and Sonny Boy."

I pulled back the cover and got up, headed for the kitchen in search of what was left of the JD from last night.

"How do you drink that nasty stuff this *early* in the morning?" she asked, following me into the kitchen while picking up articles of clothing and trash in route.

"If it's one thing I *don't* mess with, it's that hard liquor. It's a good thing I don't, considering the way you drink. I had to drag you into the bedroom. You were completely knocked out. I shoulda left your butt out here on the couch."

"And another thing," she continued, following me back into the bedroom, "You really need to clean this place up. It's a damn *mess*." Whatever. I took a gulp of what little remained in the bottle.

She continued to bust my chops about this and that, but I wasn't listening. The information about Lester and Sonny Boy had me thinking seriously about a return visit to Park Hill. Maybe the two of them could shed some light on Sue Ellen's relationship with Earl. I headed to the bathroom to take a cold shower and shave, while she tackled the mess throughout the apartment.

"I never knew you liked the Beatles" I believed she murmured, while going through a stack of albums leaning against the wall in the living room. I could barely make out what she was saying between the noise in the shower and the noise from the TV.

"Muddy Waters, Duke Ellington, *and* Frank Sinatra? Damn baby, you got some real interesting tastes in music. Can I borrow this Ray Charles record?"

"No!" I yelled over the noisy shower.

"Why not? What you gonna play'em on? *You* ain't got no record player."

"I'm buying one when I get paid next week" I yelled while turning off the shower and pulling down a towel from back of the bathroom door.

By the time I had dressed, she had transformed the apartment into something fairly livable again. The challenge for me would now be to find everything.

"I put all your records in the front closet and moved some of your clothes back to the bedroom. That way, you can put those boxes in the bedroom closet, seeing as though you don't plan on making this home."

"Is that an observation or a question?" I asked.

"I don't know...you tell me. And by the way, that's an orange shirt you got on."

"So?"

"So? Since when do a yellow tie, orange shirt and a brown suit go together?" You know what you look like?"

"Whatever..."

"And before I forget, I put all your mail inside the nightstand next to the bed. You sure do have a lot of mail from Willow Manor," she noted curiously. "That's a pretty fancy place. I got a cousin that works out there in housekeeping. I hear they pay good. I need to get *me* a job out there."

"How long have you been at the luncheonette anyway?" I asked, shifting the conversation from Willow Manor.

"Almost three years now I think. Time flies you know."

"So why do you stay?" I asked while looking through the closet for a shirt of another color.

"What else can a girl like me do? I ain't cleaning nobody's house or taking care of nobody's babies. And I *ain't working for Levi either,*" she said emphatically. "I'm just trying to save enough money to go to cosmetology school."

"Cosmo…what?" I asked.

"Fix hair."

"Right. Well what's stopping you?"

"Ain't no school down here, but there's one in Atlanta. As soon as I get the six-hundred dollars I need to sign up, you won't see me at Long's again. You wouldn't be interested in making a girl a loan would you?" she inquired with a smile.

"I think I'll take a ride over to Park Hill to see your neighbor," I said, changing the subject once again. Fortunately Danita didn't continue that line of questioning...

She had a couple of hours to kill before reporting to work, so I reluctantly gave her the apartment key to lock up and promised we'd talk later. Hopefully she wouldn't take that as an invitation to stay.

CHAPTER TWELVE

Park Hill was a working class colored community on the south side of the city. Most who lived there either worked for the local hotels, restaurants, or the furniture factory on the edge of town. The lawns were neatly manicured and the small, densely spaced homes were well maintained. There seemed to be a real sense of pride and community among the colored folks who lived on this side of town.

I parked in front of Lester's house and made a mental note to gas up on the way back to the office, cursing at the expense. Twenty-eight cents for a gallon of gas. What was this world coming to?

"Yes sir. What can I do for ya sir?" asked an elderly gentleman who opened the front door wide enough to speak, just as I was about to knock.

"Detective Monroe, Savannah Law Enforcement." I held up my badge for him to see through the narrow opening.

"I knows who you are. I saw ya last night over at Danita's. Is she all right?"

"Yeah. She's fine. I'm looking for Mr. Lester. Would that be you sir?"

"Yes sir, that's me, Officer."

"I'd like to ask you a few questions."

"Bout what?" he asked, somewhat nervously.

"I'm investigating the murder of Earl McKenna."

He stood silently for a moment, and then opened the door a little wider.

"I don't know nothing about that."

"But I understand you did some work for him and his wife. I just want to ask you a few questions, that's all." He was silent. "We can do this now or we can do it downtown. Your choice."

After a few seconds, he motioned for me to enter.

He was an older gentleman, medium build, late 60's, maybe early 70's with thinning gray hair. A pair of stripped suspenders held up a pair of baggy overalls. I entered as directed, following him as he limped slightly through his small one level home. It was neatly arranged inside and had a scent of tobacco. A small oscillating fan sat in front of an old rocking chair facing the front window. The fan didn't seem to make much of an impact on the hot and stuffy room. On one wall hung several medals attached to red, white and blue ribbons. They were armed forces' medals – maybe

Army or Marines. He led me to a screen door in the back that opened to a small porch.

After plopping down in an old rocking chair he gestured for me to sit in the chair directly across from him. He removed an old corncob from a side table and stuffed it with smoking tobacco. I likewise lit up a cigarette after removing an *Ebony* magazine from the chair before sitting down. In the distance I could see kids playing stickball on a makeshift field, happily running between clotheslines holding wet clothes held by big wooden pins. It brought back childhood memories of growing up in Queens. Memories I'd rather forget.

"Seeing as though my fan ain't working too well, we probably better off sitting out here. I swear, it's really been one hot summer, ain't it? Can't remember it being this hot this time last summer, can you?" he asked, rocking for a moment before abruptly stopping. "Pardon my manners. Can I get you something to drink, Detective? I just made a big old pitcher of sweet tea."

That did sound good, but I was here on business, not to socialize. "No thanks. I'm fine."

"So what do you need to know Detective...what you say your name is again?"

"Monroe."

"Yeah, that's right, Monroe," he chuckled. "You ain't from around these parts is ya?"

"New York, born and raised."

"Up north, huh? Yeah, I could tell. You don't seem like them other policemen around here. Only time *they* come to a colored man's house is to arrest him," he said bitterly. "An old man like me been dealing with that all my life, but times is changing though. Dr. King and them Kennedy boys fixin to change this country. Can't nobody stop'em either. You just wait and see."

"I hope you're right, sir. I'm investigating the murder of Earl McKenna, the Chief Judge. Though his wife confessed to the murder, I'm still trying to gather as much information as I can to close our investigation. I understand you've done work for them in the past. Is that right?" I pulled out my spiral pad.

He looked off into the distance, slowly rocking again and puffing on his pipe.

"Yeah, Ms. Ellen. She a nice white lady. Real nice white lady," he answered. "I guess he musta done something real bad to make Ms. Ellen do something like that. But then you never know bout some people and how they get along wit they husband or not. I never had a problem with her. She always treated me and Sonny Boy real nice."

"Did you every witness them arguing or fighting for any reason?"

"Not that I recollect. I can't recall ever seeing him. He wasn't ever there when I was working for her. He's a big time lawyer I think, probably working away from home most of the time. People like that gotta make that money you know."

"So what kind of work *did you* do for them?"

"I'm a handy man. I fix things. Little things, big things. I can do electrical, plumbing, all kinda stuff. As a matter of fact Detective..." He paused for a moment and scratched his head.

"Monroe."

"Yeah, right, Monroe. If you ever need something done at your house, let me know. I'm your man."

"I'll keep that in mind." I took a drag and exhaled. "So how long have you been working for them?"

"Off and on, maybe three, four years or so, I think."

"When was the last time you were there?"

"Let's see…bout a week ago I think. My boy and me, we put in a new furnace in that kitchen of theirs. Now that there's some kitchen. I ain't never seen a kitchen that big before."

"Did you notice anything unusual going on between the two of them?"

"You mean Ms. Ellen and her husband?"

"Yeah. Were they getting along?"

Suddenly, a rather strange look came across his face.

"You wouldn't be related to Mr. Ricky Monroe that run that gas station down on Columbus Avenue would ya?"

"I don't think so, no."

"Damn if you don't favor him a lot," he chuckled, slapping his knee. "I tell you one thing though, that man sho don't know nothing bout fixing cars."

"Right…did Sue Ellen ever say anything about any problems they were having?" I asked, redirecting the conversation.

"Problems? What kinda problems?" he asked.

"Domestic abuse." He stared at me, appearing somewhat confused.

"Did you ever notice any signs that he might be beating her?" I asked.

"Well now, come to think of it, a couple of weeks ago she did have a few bruises on her arm. She said she fell." He took the pipe out of his mouth and shook his head. "But a fall don't make no bruises like that."

"A couple of weeks ago?"

"Yeah, bout," he answered as I jotted a few notes in my pad.

"Is there anything else you can remember that might help me understand why Sue Ellen would say she committed this crime?"

He continued to rock while he puffed on his pipe, then stopped for a second and scratched his head. "No sir, not that I can think of."

He didn't seem to know anything of much help but regardless, I had to close the loop with everyone connected to the victim and to his wife.

"Is Sonny Boy around?"

"Sonny? Naw, he ain't here. He work over at the Savoy Lounge on Greenbrier, for Mr. Levi."

"Is he there now?"

"Can't say. That boy keeps all kinda strange hours. You know how these young kids are."

"Ever seen this before?" I asked, handing him the silver medallion.

"Mighty nice piece," he said, slowly rubbing his fingers across the image of St. Peter. He turned it over and his face blanched. He looked as if he had just seen a ghost.

"Do you know who KJ is?"

He hesitated for a moment, and then shook his head without looking up.

I could tell he was lying. It was the same reaction I had gotten from Sue Ellen during questioning.

"Mind if I use your telephone?"

He stood up slowly, leaning on the rocking chair to maintain his balance. "Ain't got no phone here, but there's one on the corner at the gas station," he answered before opening the screen door and stepping back into his house. Once inside, he locked it, leaving me outside on his back porch.

Why would he lie? I'm sure I saw a phone while walking through the house.

I left my card on his rocking chair with a phone number in the unlikely event he remembered something that might be valuable to the investigation. I walked down several wobbly steps on the side of the porch towards the front of the house and back to the car.

After filling up at the gas station, I put in a call to Bobby, gave him a quick update, and asked him to meet me at the Savoy Lounge in a half hour.

CHAPTER THIRTEEN

By the time I got to the Savoy, Bobby was already standing out front, angrily pacing back and forth. I pulled up behind the squad car and got out, expecting to get a lecture about my disappearing act over the last few days. He had a concerned look on his face as he stood in front of the club entrance with both hands on his hips. He looked pissed.

"Where in the world you been Boy?"

"It's a long story."

"Well I got all day, so you best start talking."

"Can it wait?"

"No. It can't wait," he answered taking off his fedora and using his other hand to wipe the sweat from his forehead. "You trying my patience. You can't just disappear from the office and not check in with your partner! Nobody knew where in the world you were. What the heck am I supposed to tell the Chief?"

"Look, I'm sorry. I know I got some explaining to do, but right now we need to talk to anyone who might be connected somehow to the Judge and his wife. Just trust me on this one," I pleaded. "Okay?"

He looked down at the sweltering sidewalk, still apparently upset, and then put his fedora back on.

"All right. This better be good. I'm going to cut you some slack for the moment, but you got some explaining to do later," he warned, appearing to calm down a little.

"By the way, what *did* you tell the Chief?" I asked.

"I told him you had to take care of some family business," he answered. "May the good Lord forgive me for lying" he mumbled, looking up at the sky and shaking his head.

"Thanks. I owe you one." Actually I had been taking care of business, just not family business.

"Yeah, whatever," he responded. "Satan never sleeps."

CHAPTER FOURTEEN

The Savoy Lounge was part speakeasy, part restaurant, and a few other things besides. It was an old converted warehouse at the end of Greenbrier Street that sat next to, of all things a Baptist church. Owned and operated by Levi Bookins, or "Mr. Levi," it was the only place in town for colored folk to gather, let their hair down and have a good time. Some say he ran the numbers racket in the colored community and even dabbled in drugs and prostitution. Others regarded him as a local hero - a colored businessman who understood how to make a dollar. One thing *was* for sure; if you wanted or needed anything on this side of town, chances are you'd have to go through "Mr. Levi" to get it.

We walked up to the front door, knocked, and waited patiently in the hot afternoon sun. A constant stream of cars with radios blaring drove down the narrow one-way street while a group of men wearing white gloves removed a body from a hearse in the church's driveway. No one seemed to notice us. Maybe they were used to seeing cops in front of the Savoy.

"These boys don't like cops and they're packing so keep ya cool and for God's sake… remember to keep your back to the door, all right?"

"Are you kidding? We're talking about some low life country hoods not, the New York mafia."

"Just remember what I'm telling ya okay?"

We knocked again, waiting impatiently in the hot sun for what seemed like an eternity. I'm sure they knew a couple of cops were standing outside their door. They were just making us wait. I'm not sure about Bobby, but I had no intention of leaving until I could talk to Sonny Boy. Eventually a slider abruptly opened revealing a pair of suspicious eyes staring at us through a narrow opening.

"Can I help you?" a deep baritone voice behind the slider asked. I held up my badge.

"We're here to see Bookins."

"You mean *Mister* Levi," the voice responded emphatically.

"Yeah, whatever," I answered. It was uncomfortably hot and my patience was wearing thin.

The slider shut abruptly. We stood there staring at each other, not exactly sure what to expect. Hopefully we weren't back to square one. Just as I was about to knock again the door opened slowly. A huge, sharply dressed goon, about six-five, maybe two hundred pounds motioned for us to follow him. He was sporting a white wide brim hat and wore a baggy light blue linen suit with white loafers. It was hard not to laugh. Southern-style gangster chic, I suppose.

We followed him as directed through a long dark corridor eventually walking into a large ballroom. A small stage with a drum kit sat at one end of the ballroom and an enormous wooden bar stretched across the length of the wall at the other end. In between were large round tables draped in white linen tablecloths. Fancy chandeliers hanging from a vaulted ceiling created a soft subdued mood. The smell of fried chicken and collard greens seeped into the ballroom from a kitchen somewhere in the building.

Even at this hour of the day, several people sat at the bar playing cards and taking shots – most likely moonshine. Much to my surprise it was quite a classy place, similar to what you'd expect to find in Harlem or on the South Side of Chicago.

All conversation at the bar abruptly stopped and all eyes followed us as we followed our escort through the ballroom. He led us up a set of steps directly behind the bar to a second level. At the top of the stairs he pointed to a door at the end of the hall. Another goon stopped us there.

"What business you got with Mr. Levi?" he asked.

"We need to talk to one of his employees."

"Let 'em through," yelled a voice from inside the room. He stepped aside as told, allowing us to enter a large, brightly lit room. Its exposed beams and brick walls were reminders of its past life as an old warehouse. He sat behind a large dark mahogany desk in front of a bay window. From a seated position he appeared to be rather short with a thin build and a large Afro. He wore a shiny silver sharkskin suit with a black shirt and a bright red tie.

He certainly didn't live up to the badass image I had envisioned. As a matter of fact, he looked more like a Times Square pimp than a businessman. Sitting on the edge of his desk was an attractive young colored lady sporting a blond wig and wearing a tight black, low cut dress with matching fish net stockings. Well at least he had good taste. He motioned for her to leave. She smiled and winked at me on her way out.

"So what brings you boys out here on a hot ass day like today?" he asked, crushing the remains of his half smoked cigar in an expensive-looking ashtray. "Didn't we take care of business last week?" he asked, looking at Bobby. I wasn't sure what he meant by that question. Bobby remained silent.

"What business?" I asked curiously.

He smiled at the goon who had stepped in front of the doorway and shut the door behind us.

"Well I'll be damned. You hear that Bo?" he asked, smiling at another goon standing to his left.

"What business?" he said, laughing while attempting to imitate my New York accent.

"Yeah Mr. Levi. I hear that," answered Bo.

He began laughing uncontrollably, causing Bo to laugh also before suddenly slamming his fist down on the desk. His big grin suddenly turned angry and intimidating. I looked at Bobby, who had nervously dropped his left hand down by his side. Our backs were to the door.

"You the new kid from up north, ain't ya?" he asked, carefully unwrapping a new cigar, still looking me dead in the eyes. He bit off the end and spit it in my direction. "So the boys downtown are sending you to do their dirty work now, huh?"

"I got no idea what you're talking about Bookins," I answered nervously.

He smiled and removed a gold lighter from the center drawer of his desk, using it to light his cigar. Once lit, he took a long draw and exhaled smoke rings towards the ceiling. He nodded to Bo who walked across the room and opened a wall safe hidden behind a portrait of Martin Luther King.

"You fucking cops are sucking my ass dry. You know that, right? Business ain't been shit lately. People been scared to come out at night ever since that nigger got shot downstairs. I can't move no *shine*." He took another draw on his cigar and blew the smoke in my direction. "Don't matter no how. I got a shipment of that psychedelic shit coming in from up north the end of this week. I got people on the street ready to move it too. I believe ya'll white boys call that *diversifying*," he said slowly, emphasizing each syllable of the word with a big smile.

Bo removed a small brown paper bag from the safe and tossed it at me. I caught it with my right hand and opened it just enough to look inside. I looked at Bobby. He looked away, avoiding eye contact. It was pretty obvious what the deal was.

I tossed the paper bag back at Levi, which just missed his desk and hit the floor, scattering what appeared to be thousands of dollars in one hundred dollar bills.

"I didn't come here for this."

"No?" answered a puzzled Levi.

"I came here to see Sonny Boy."

He looked at Bo. Both seemed surprised and confused. He instructed Bo to quickly gather up the cash and return it to the safe.

Relieved, he leaned back in his big leather chair. His stern face suddenly reverted to a big wide grin again.

"Well damn, why didn't you say so? How bout a cigar?" he asked, holding up a large wooden box. "Cubans…the best."

They had red labels at the ends, just like the one in Bobby's trailer home. I was certainly tempted, but declined.

"So what you wanna know bout that young nigger?"

"I'm told he works for you. What exactly does he do?"

"A little bit of this, little bit of that…you know…errands," he answered. "What he do?"

"I'd like to ask him a few questions about the McKenna murder."

"The McKenna murder? Damn. Now *that* was some crazy ass shit," proffered Levi, blowing smoke rings up at the ceiling after taking a long draw.

"That shit wouldn't happen to me. I don't mess wit no *crazy* bitches."

Bo chuckled to himself. "That's right. Mr. Levi don't mess wit no crazy bitches."

"Is he here?" I asked impatiently.

"Who? Sonny? Shit, that nigger gone. He left just a few minutes before you got here."

"Any idea where he went?"

"Damn if I know, but wherever that nigger went, he sho left in a hurry. Maybe he knew you was coming," he answered, smiling at Bo. "You see, us colored folk got us a *sixth sense.* We know when *the man* is coming."

"That's right Mr. Levi, we know," mimicked a grinning Bo.

He'd probably gotten a call from Lester. I should've known better.

"So what he got to do with that murder anyway?" asked Levi.

"It's standard procedure to talk to anyone who may have been in contract with the victim. We understand he did some work for the Judge and his wife."

"Oh yeah. You right. He used to help out his daddy. He always talked about how nice that house was." He took another draw on his cigar.

"One of these days I'm gonna get me a house just like that up there with all y'all white folks. You just wait and see. I hope y'all like the smell of barbeque," he chuckled.

"Yeah. Mr. Levi gonna have him a house like that…and we gonna be barbequing every day" Bo added with a childish grin.

"Do you know anything about their missing daughter?" I asked. "I'm told she disappeared about a year ago. Did he ever say anything about that?"

"Yeah. I remember that - pretty little white girl. They had cops all over town looking for her. They even searched this part of town…can you imagine that? Colored girls run away every day. Cops don't care about *them*."

"Did Sonny Boy have any contact with her?"

"I think Sonny Boy was sweet on her. He talked about her a few times. I told that fool he need to watch that shit. You know what they do to a nigger who mess with a white woman *down here*? This ain't the North."

"If you see him, you tell him I'm looking for him."

"Well I most certainly will Detective. Always glad to be of assistance to our boys downtown," he answered with a big grin. "I believe you boys know how to find your way back out."

Savannah was a small town. Sonny Boy may have slipped through my fingers this time but it was just a matter of time before I'd find him. At least it hadn't been a total waste of time. I had gotten to finally meet the infamous Mr. Levi and in the process, uncovered a nasty little secret about the Savannah Police Department.

I turned around and headed for the door, walking right past Bobby who looked at the floor, avoiding eye contact with me.

"By the way," Levi yelled, just as I reached the door. "What's your name?"

"Monroe. Tyler Monroe."

"Nice suit Monroe."

I waited outside for bobby to exit the lounge and then followed him as he walked quickly, head down, back to his car. Protruding from his left coat pocket was what appeared to be a brown bag closely resembling the one I had refused to take from Levi.

"What the hell's going on?" I asked.

"What does it look like?" he shot back. "Don't you go judging me, Youngblood. You don't understand *nothing*!" he yelled, breathing heavy while fumbling with the keys to unlock the car door. "Times is changing. Sometimes you got to play ball in order to survive."

"Is bribery somewhere in that Bible of yours? You got a verse for that too?"

"Look, I've been working and living on a civil servant's salary for thirty years and you know what I got to show for it? A trailer that's about to fall apart and a ten-year-old station wagon. That's what. You want a verse? How about *the Lord be magnified, who delights in the prosperity of his servant.*

"It's simple," he continued more quietly, suddenly aware of a small group of colored folks watching from across the street. "We look the other way and Levi takes care of us. Who cares, as long as they keep that stuff on their side of town?"

"That's bullshit and you know it."

'Maybe so, but you need to wake up and smell the bullshit boy. It's everywhere. You can't stop it. Why should we be any different? If you got any sense, you'll keep your mouth shut and get a piece of it too," he said wiping the sweat running down his forehead with the back of his hand.

Disgusted, I stared at him for a moment before slowly walking back to my car. Once inside, I sat silently for a few minutes, trying to process what had just happened. Against my better judgment I reached underneath the front seat and removed the flask I had hidden there. I had made it to day two without a drink. Unfortunately that's where it would end.

CHAPTER FIFTEEN

The Chief had already finished his daily briefing by the time I checked in the next morning. Even though his office door was shut, I could still hear muffled voices inside. Bobby said nothing, avoiding eye contact with me and nervously fumbling with a stack of folders. Pete and Andy appeared occupied with paperwork and failed to acknowledge my presence as well. A small sealed envelope lay next to my phone. I opened it, took a quick look at the note inside and discreetly stuffed it into my pocket.

"Somebody slid that under the door this morning" Bobby said, referring to the envelope. "That's probably not a good idea around here," he added, looking in the direction of Pete and Andy.

"So what did I miss?" I asked.

"Sue Ellen's been moved to the state women's prison outside of Savannah. At this point no sentencing date has been set. The autopsy confirmed the cause of death as multiple blows to the head."

"And a murder weapon?" I asked.

"None found," he answered. That would confirm our theory about the dolls. It certainly looked like an open and shut case, but something just didn't feel right. At this point it made sense to keep quiet about the additional evidence we had gathered until we could dig deeper for concrete evidence. We still needed to talk to Sonny.

For the moment however, I had a date with the Feds.

"I need to grab the squad car for about an hour. I've got a few errands I need to take care of. You okay with that?" I asked Bobby.

"Okay, but remember we're pretty backed up with stuff we need to investigate" he replied.

"Got it. I'll be back shortly.

The Starlight was a seedy motel on the west end of town that catered to lowlifes and bums. It was notorious for drug dealing, prostitution and Saturday night shootings. It had three floors accessible from a set of stairs on each end of the building. I left the squad car at the TEXACO station across the street for an oil change and quickly crossed the street, hoping not to be seen. Fortunately a desk clerk stationed inside a small booth out front appeared to be sleep as I passed on my way to the rear stairway.

As stated in the note left under the office door earlier, Room 22C was on the second floor directly across from a public bathroom. I could smell the stench of urine from the ground floor.

The heat and humidity made it even worse. The motel was a real dump. I knocked once on the door as instructed. Shortly a voice on the other side directed me to enter.

"Have a seat," said the voice from the other side of the room.

I complied, sitting in a rickety wooden chair next to a small table that now separated of us. A small desk lamp had been strategically positioned to shine directly in my face, making it almost impossible to see the individual on the other side of the table. The curtains were closed and a mattress had been placed in front of the window to make the room as dark as possible. The room had a mildewed odor, made worse by moving air compliments of a noisy ceiling fan that didn't provide any relief from the heat.

"It's been a while since we last spoke Mr. Monroe. How are you adjusting to your new *home*?"

"It sucks."

"It can't be any worse than that cesspool New York." I couldn't see his face but I could tell he was smiling.

"The agency needs an update. Our sources say there's a scheduled drop sometime next week. What's the word on the street?"

"We'll get to that in a moment. In the meantime there are a few things *I'd* like to clear up first."

"Such as?" he asked.

"Such as leaving notes for me at the office. That's a *big* problem. I don't care how you do it, but from here on out you need to find some other way to communicate with me.

"Number two. When do I get outta this shithole? It's been six goddamn months already!"

"Unfortunately I can't answer that question at this time" he said. "For now, just stick to the plan."

"That's the same damn answer I got last month" I shot back.

"You're not exactly in a position to bargain Mr. Monroe, so I suggest you stick to the agreement and deliver your end of the deal. Do I make myself clear?" he asked.

"The drop Mr. Monroe. What about the drop?" he asked again. I took a deep breath to calm down before answering.

"It's being moved through the colored neighborhoods. From what I understand it's a pretty sizable shipment of amphetamines and psychedelics coming from Atlanta by way of New York. Why not just cut it off at the source?" I asked. That would be the logical thing to do.

"Why? Because we need to know how it moves, specifically the distribution points, the cash flow, and most importantly who's involved. Until now it's been confined only to parts of the Northeast and California. Now it's spreading to the South. Before long, it'll be all over the country. The agency believes it's a Russian instigated conspiracy to weaken our country. It's our job to crush this cancer before it gains irreversible momentum."

"So we allow this poison to spread through these communities just for the purpose of *gathering information*? What justifies that? We're talking about destroying people's lives here."

"That's not for you to question," he answered abruptly. "Besides, why would you care? It's just a bunch of niggers, right?" I sat there silently, both hands tightly gripping the sides of the wooden chair to avoid doing something I might later regret.

He tossed a pad in my direction. "I need dealers' names and drop locations."

"What about the locals?" he asked. I removed a Marlboro from the pack and lit it before answering.

"It's a weekly pickup. Most of the force is involved but I'm not sure about the Chief."

"Write it down" he demanded. I complied, jotting down specific details for the next few minutes while referring from time to time with the notes in my note pad.

"So now what?" I asked after finally completing the documentation and tossing it on the table between us.

"We need to know who running the operation down here."

"Bookins," I replied.

"Bookins?" he said, somewhat amused. "Hell, we already know about Bookins. He's just a small time two-bit hood. We want to know who's supplying *him*." It was obvious where this conversation was headed. The only other organization capable of handling an interstate operation this big was the mob. I stood up and shoved the chair under the table between us.

"That wasn't a part of the original agreement," I said, defiantly.

"I think it would be in your best interest to *sit down* Mr. Monroe," he said coolly. He scanned the names on the sheet before placing them in a folder. "If you recall, we made a deal. Risk is just a part of the job. It's all very simple. You deliver what we want and you get what you want."

"Both you *and* the agency can kiss my ass!" I was done with this assignment and this city. I headed for the door…next stop New York City.

"Our Intel *said* you were highly-strung and impulsive," he insinuated as I unlatched the door, "but very good at what you do. Seems they were right. Think about it Mr. Monroe, what exactly do you have to go back *to*? With your record, no one's going to touch you."

Unfortunately he was right. I *had* burned a lot of bridges in my career to get to this point.

"I would *strongly* advise you reconsider, Mr. Monroe. No one is going to force you to do anything. However, you know how to reach me when you come to your senses."

Disgusted, I opened the door to leave.

"And by the way, please give my regards to Ms. Albright," he smirked. "I'm sure she's getting the best possible care at Willow Manor. It's a very nice place. It must be tough to afford her care on a salary like yours."

I didn't turn around, but I could tell the son-of-a-bitch had a smile on his face. How in the hell did they know about *that*?

"Surprised?" he asked. "Don't forget who you're dealing with. There's very little you can hide from us. Just stick to the agreement, Mr. Monroe. It'll be over soon enough."

I stood in the open doorway for a second more, before slamming the door and heading toward the steps at the other end of the hall. I pondered my options – few if any weighed in my favor. What had I gotten myself into?

In hindsight leaving through the front entrance had been a dumb move. A patrol car had stopped a car across the street to issue a ticket. To avoid being seen coming out of the motel, I walked quickly, head down, in the opposite direction away from the gas station. I made a quick detour inside a small grocery store and made small talk with the cutie behind the counter while checking the storefront window for signs of the patrol car. Minutes later the patrol car passed by. The glare on the window from the sun however, made it impossible to see the driver. Hopefully whoever it was hadn't seen me. Or had they?

I waited for a few minutes before backtracking to the gas station to pick up the car. While there, I called Bobby and informed him that I was on my way back to the office to pick him up for lunch.

CHAPTER SIXTEEN

By now it was close to noon and the place was filled with all the lunchtime regulars. Danita was up front taking an order as we slowly made our way through the crowd. I was careful not to look in her direction. Pete and Andy were seated at their usual table. We found an empty table in a quiet section in the back.

"I guess I owe you an apology," Bobby said after removing his glasses and placing them in front of him on the table. "Do I feel bad about it? Yeah I do but when you get my age your priorities change. Sometimes you just gotta do what you gotta do to get by. Know what I mean?" It still seemed completely out of sync with all the religious stuff he had been spouting to me.

"No need to explain anything to me, partner. As a matter of fact, I've been thinking a lot about what you suggested. Are you sure this thing is safe?" I asked.

"As long as you do what you're told and don't get greedy" he answered.

"I could really use the extra money. How do I get in?" I asked in order to satisfy my secret deal with the Feds.

"You sure about this?" he said, peering at me with a look of surprise.

"Yeah," I answered, avoiding eye contact.

He sighed with relief and leaned across the table within a few inches of my face. "We can't stop this kinda stuff," he whispered. "It's over our heads. We just keep our mouths shut and take our cuts. You won't get rich, but it's a nice little piece of change."

I felt like a lousy sellout, but what choice did I have?

For the next hour he provided the details, specifically the kind of drugs getting into the city and how it was being distributed on the streets. The operation was far more sophisticated than even I had suspected. According to him there were only a few cops involved. They were taking bribes to look the other way. In return, they received ten percent off the top weekly but were pressuring Levi for more. Levi wanted to expand into the white neighborhoods, but that meant moving in on someone else's territory. Exactly whose territory, Bobby wouldn't say. It was also unclear *who* the man at the top was. Either he didn't know or was reluctant to share that piece of information.

"Refill on the coffee, sir?" Danita asked, interrupting our conversation. We were so engaged that I hadn't noticed her standing there. She smiled at Bobby but ignored me.

"Yeah, and bring me a piece of that pecan pie. Man, it's granny-slappin' good. Add a scoop of vanilla ice cream on top too. You want anything partner? It's on me today."

I shook my head no. I just didn't seem to have an appetite this afternoon.

"You got it sir. Coming right out."

She turned and headed for the counter stopping for a moment to chat with a teenager standing near the cash register. He wore an old baggy tee shirt, faded blue dungarees and black high-top tennis shoes. He was probably eighteen maybe nineteen, sporting a big afro. He tossed a stack of newspapers on top of the counter.

"How you doing Sonny Boy?" she asked, speaking loud enough for us to hear above the lunchtime chatter. "I ain't seen you in a month a' Sundays. How's Mr. Lester doing?"

I knew I'd eventually catch up with him and today was my lucky day. Without a word I gave a slight nod to Bobby, who could tell what I was thinking. If only she could hold his attention long enough for me to get closer. I kept my eyes on him while slowly moving my chair away from the table. In the process I accidentally bumped a gentleman passing behind me causing him to spill the drink he was carrying. Sonny Boy made eye contact with me for a split second during the commotion. Sensing something was wrong, he bolted for the door. I guess he had that sixth sense Levi had spoken of after all.

I took off after him, almost knocking Danita to the floor as I ran by. Chaos erupted as he pushed, shoved, and jumped over damn near everything between him and the door. I'd never seen a human move that fast in my entire life.

He darted out the door and up the street leaving a trail of dropped newspapers behind. I followed, doing my best to keep up, but I was simply no match for this kid in the afternoon heat. In just a matter of seconds, he had disappeared.

"Looking for that nigger?" yelled an old woman on the corner. "He went that-a-way," she said, pointing in the direction of the Greyhound station a block away.

Out of breath, I quickly crossed the street in that direction and took the side entrance into the terminal.

The Greyhound bus terminal was a small station on Main Street directly across from the Rialto Theater. I'd driven passed it several times but never had a reason to go inside until now. Unlike the new bus station uptown, this one served "colored only" - another ugly example of the segregated South.

It was a busy place that was hotter on the inside than the sweltering heat outside. Large fans along each wall didn't help, nor did the smell of exhaust fumes lingering inside the terminal from buses parked outside adding to the discomfort.

Old ladies wearing big straw hats carried suitcases held together with rope and restless children chased each other around the station. Many waited in the center of the terminal listening for gate announcements over an intercom, before hurrying to the announced departure door. The poor quality of the intercom system made it damn near impossible to understand what gate they were announcing. It was organized disorder and the perfect place to blend in and disappear. That son of a bitch had lucked out. Nonetheless, I pushed my way through the crowd slowly hoping I might get lucky.

"Sorry to bother you Mister, but can you tell me where the Birmingham gate is?" asked a frail elderly colored man looking somewhat confused. He was neatly dressed in a light brown suit that seemed a size too large. He carried a large suitcase in each hand.

"All the gates are marked," I answered, pointing to the signs above each door. "Just look for the one that says Birmingham or wait for the gate announcement over the speaker."

"Yes 'em, I understands that Sir, but…that's a might difficult when ya blind." That explained the sunglasses inside the terminal. I didn't mind helping the old man but time was of the essence. The fact that Sonny Boy ran meant he knew something. I just couldn't afford to lose him *a second time.* Reluctantly, I grabbed one of his suitcases and took him by the hand, hoping I wouldn't regret this.

Each gate had a line of passengers waiting to board. The longest lines were for Atlanta, Macon, and Memphis. The Washington, DC gate was empty, but the gate door leading to the bus had been opened. That was unusual. Next to the DC gate was the Birmingham gate. There were only a handful of people waiting in that line. I led him over to the gate.

"This is your gate sir. Wait right here. It should be boarding in a few minutes." I placed the other suitcase down by his side.

"I sho do appreciate this Mister. That's very kind of you," he said, setting down his suitcase and extending his hand in gratitude.

"You're lucky I decided to come back."

He smiled. "Ain't no such think as luck. God blesses those with kindness in their hearts. What's meant to be will always find its way," he said quietly. "Remember that."

Having done my good deed for today, I quickly resumed my search. Instead of the ticket window, I decided to check out the open gate door for the DC bus. Those doors are not usually opened until boarding is about to begin. I stepped outside and searched the area around the bus. The bus door was open but no one was board, not even the driver. Curious, I boarded and slowly walked down the aisle, carefully examining each seat row by row. About a third of the way down I spotted a motionless figure crouched between a row of seats to my right.

Exhausted and overcome by the heat, I sat down on the other side of the aisle, pushing my seat into a reclining position. Damn that felt good. I lit a Marlboro.

"Where'd you learn to run like that kid?" I asked, taking a nice long drag. No answer. I waited.

"Come in handy when you colored," finally came a voice from the other side of the aisle. It was the first honest answer I'd heard in a while.

"You're a real hard person to find Sonny Boy. You know that?"

"Why you looking for me? I didn't do nothing Officer," he responded.

"I never said you *did.* I just want to ask you a few questions about the Judge and his wife that's all. You don't need to be afraid of me."

"You mean you ain't gonna arrest me?"

"Not unless you give me a good reason to."

He got up slowly from the floor and reluctantly sat in the seat directly across from me, still looking at me suspiciously. He was missing one sneaker.

"Smoke?" I asked, reaching inside my coat for my pack of Marlboros.

"No sir."

"Take my advice kid, don't ever start."

"What you wanna know from me?" he asked, watching me carefully.

"Tell me what you know about the Judge and his wife." He pushed his chair into a reclining position just as I had done.

"Well, me and Lester…that's my paw, we just did some work for them at their house," he began. "I just come along on the weekends ever now and then when my paw needed help.

"What type of work?"

"Fixing stuff, painting, yard work… stuff like that. Most of the time I'm delivering papers or working for Mr. Levi."

"You ever see him hit his wife?"

"No sir, but I know they used to fuss a lot."

"How'd you know that?"

"She always complained to me and Lester bout how he say it was *her* fault their daughter ran away."

"What did he mean by that?"

"I don't know."

"Did you know their daughter?" I asked, taking down a few notes.

"I used to see her sometimes when we was over there working."

"How well did you know her?" I asked. He shifted nervously in his seat, apparently uncomfortable with the question.

"She was different."

"How so?"

"She liked colored people."

"Liked?"

"Yeah, I mean…she wasn't prejudiced or nothing like that, you know? She was always talking about civil rights and taking part in marches and stuff. She was a good person."

"Any idea what happened to her?"

He looked out the window without answering.

"I'm told she got into a fight with her folks over some boy at school. Now that wouldn't be you would it?"

"Me? Hell no!" he retorted, surprised at the question.

"Where you from mister? They don't allow us to go to the same schools down here. That boy you talking bout – he was on the football team. She was crazy bout him. He all she ever talked about."

"What's his name?"

"Clyde," he answered, scratching his head. "But it don't matter no how. She broke up wit him after she caught him messing around with her girlfriend. She told me she was gonna get back at him."

"How did she plan on doing that?"

He gazed out the window silently. I could tell he knew more that he was willing to say. A few pieces were starting to come together, but there were still gaps. It might be a good idea to talk to this kid Clyde if I could find him.

"Freeze you little black son of a bitch!" yelled a familiar voice, walking down the isle with his gun pointed directly at the kid.

"Git yo black ass up outta that seat you little piece of shit!" he yelled, his gun now pointed directly at the kid, who slowly got up from his seat with both hands raised over his head.

"What you want with me? I didn't *do* nothing, I didn't *do nothing!*" he pleaded.

"Shut the hell up and keep both them hands up where I can see 'em!" Pete wiped sweat from his forehead with his free hand and stepped closer. His gun was now pointed directly at the kid's head.

"I bet you bout to shit yo pants ain't ya Boy?" he asked, breathing heavily while stepping close enough to place the barrel of his gun against the boy's temple. Visibly shaken and scared to death, the kid didn't say a word. I had no idea what was about to happen but one thing *was* certain– this situation had the potential to get real ugly. At that range, a single shot would be the last thing the kid would ever remember. I just hoped like hell he wouldn't make any sudden moves.

I got up slowly, placing both hands in plain sight on top of the seat in front of me.

I kept my eyes on Pete.

"Everything's under control Pete" I explained, trying hard not to make any sudden moves. "He's not going anywhere so just *calm down* and put the gun away, *okay?"* He looked at me but kept his pistol aimed directly at the boy's head.

"You can start by telling me what the *hell* is going on. What'd that nigger steal in the restaurant?"

"Nothing" I answered.

"Nothing?" he asked, looking at me, apparently confused.

"Yeah, nothing. I thought he was someone else."

"Someone else? Well if he didn't do nothing, why'd he run like a bat outta hell?"

"He was scared, that's why. It was just a case of mistaken identity," I answered, eyes still fixed on him. He had a strange look on his face. I wasn't sure whether he was buying my explanation or not.

"Ain't I seen you somewhere before Boy?" he asked.

Sonny shook his head no, but Pete continued to stare at the kid.

"You look mighty familiar" he continued, still holding the barrel against the side of the kid's head.

"Hell, you know all niggers look alike, right?" I pleaded, hoping he'd listen.

His eyes shifted between the two of us, still pointing his pistol at the boy's head. The next few seconds felt like hours as the three of us stood there motionless and silent. Finally, he broke into a wide grin and lowered his pistol. I let out a quiet sigh of relief. I'm sure the kid did too.

"For once, I guess you right, Big City. All them niggers do look alike,"he smirked, placing his pistol back in the holster on his hip. "So what you think we ought a do with this here spook?"

"Let 'em go. He ain't the one I'm looking for."

"You sure bout that?" he asked.

"Yeah, he's too short." He took another long look at Sonny Boy.

"Alright Big City, he's yours," he said, then pointed his finger at Sonny.

"But if I ever catch your black ass around that restaurant again, I'll send you back to ya momma in a pine box. You hear me boy?"

"Yes'm," he answered thankfully, still looking down.

"No need to mention this to the Chief," he said, looking me directly in the eyes.

"Never happened," I answered. As he turned and headed back down the aisle I could hear the kid say under his breath, "Next time red neck, next time."

We both sat down finally, relieved. A good smoke would really hit the spot now, but I was all out of cigarettes. I took out a pack of gum instead.

"Juicy fruit?" I asked. He reached over and took a piece, unwrapped it and shoved it in his mouth. We both sat quietly for a few minutes, emotionally drained.

"So you really think we all look alike?" he asked, breaking the silence. "Cause if you ask me, I think all ya'll look alike..."

I couldn't contain my laughter at that point, causing him to start laughing too. It felt good to release the tension. "I don't understand why you lied to him?" he asked, shifting the mood back to a more serious tone.

"What lie?"

"You know…that I was the wrong person. Why was you trying to protect me?"

"Well it *was* true wasn't it? You *hadn't* done anything. Besides, I didn't want to see you get hurt. That guy's a real asshole."

"They *all* assholes if you ask me," he angrily retorted, kicking the seat in front of him. "They bother us all the time for *no* reason. Last week they arrested my cousin Kenny. He didn't do a damn thing. They claimed he was selling pills, but he wasn't selling nothing. They took him in the alley and beat him up real bad. They was just looking for an excuse to beat up on somebody. That ain't right." We both sat for a moment. Finally he turned around and looked me in the eyes.

"Can I ask you a question, Mister?"

"Sure."

"Why ya'll hate us so much? What did we do to y'all? I mean, it's gotta be something we did, right?" There was a genuine sense of pain in his voice. It was a question this country needed to ask itself.

"It's complicated," I answered, wishing I had a better answer. "I know that's a real cop-out but…"

He looked at his reflection in the window as a tear rolled down the side of his face.

"Can't run from it," he said sadly. "Where you gonna go? It's the same everywhere." He wiped his eyes with the back of his hand. I knew exactly how he felt.

"Life isn't fair, but that doesn't mean you should give up," I said, sympathetic.

"I want me a nice Cadillac like Mr. Levi got. I want nice clothes and fine women just like him, and I'm gonna do what I gotta do to get all of it too. Believe that," he said, his voice suddenly rising. "Mr. Levi... now *he* get *respect.* Cops don't mess with *him*!"

"He's nothing more than a two-bit hustler. You don't want to be like him. What kind of a man sells poison to his *own people*?" He appeared unfazed by that comment.

"So what am I supposed to do? Wait on tables? Clean white folk houses? That might be all right for old niggers like my paw, but us young'uns...*we ain't doing that shit no more*!" Unfortunately he had a point. Times *were* changing.

Before our conversation could continue, we were startled by a knock on the window. To our relief however, it was Bobby. He walked to the front of the bus and entered looking disheveled, hot, and tired.

"For Christ's sake, Monroe. I been looking all over for you boy. If it wasn't for Pete, I woulda never found ya. Well I guess all's not lost," he grumbled, looking at Sonny Boy. "At least I see you finally caught up with our little friend. Damn if that boy don't move faster than grass through a cow's ass." He tossed Sonny Boy his missing sneaker.

"Yeah, it's been a real blast," I sighed, emotionally drained. I turned to Sonny Boy. "We'll talk again real soon young man, okay? In the meantime do me a favor, try to stay outta trouble." At this point I was drained, having had enough excitement for one day.

"Did you get anything worthwhile outta him?" Bobby whispered, and I pointed to the door. He got the message and we both walked back down the aisle without saying a word.

"Hey Mister!" Sonny yelled, as we were about to exit the bus.

"Yeah?"

"You pretty cool for a white boy," he said. "I owe you one."

I turned to Bobby, who looked confused.

"It's a long story."

CHAPTER SEVENTEEN

Having lost our appetite because of all the lunchtime excitement, we decided to pay a visit to the city's Office of Vital Records. Something Sonny Boy had said on the bus stuck in my head and I needed to check it out. On the drive over, I briefed Bobby on my talk with Sonny Boy and our run in with Pete. He didn't seem too surprised, but suggested I inform the Chief about the incident on the bus. Although I hated his guts, I had promised Pete it would remain between us. Who knows? One day it might buy me a favor.

As usual, Bobby knew all the short cuts, so our ride over was brief. The County Clerk's office had recently moved from City Hall to the back of the old Post Office next door. We entered the building and followed a few hand-written signs taped to the walls directing us to the second floor. There were four or five customers waiting at the reception desk when we got there.

"Hey Gladys," said Bobby, walking up to the front desk, ignoring those already in line. "How you doing gal?"

Gladys took off her reading glasses, put down the form she was reviewing, and looked up. She was an older lady, perhaps in her late fifties, with short silver hair.

"Hey *stranger.* Since we moved you don't come around to see me," she said, smiling at Bobby. "Don't you like me no more?"

"Well now look who's talking...I ain't seen you in church in a month of Sundays," he replied with a big smile. "You know what they say - don't wait til it's too late."

"Don't you go worrying bout me ya hear? So...who's your friend?" Gladys inquired.

"This here's Tyler. Tyler Monroe. He's new. I'm surprised you haven't met him by now."

"You must be the one from New York City," she said, looking me up and down.

"Yes ma'am."

"I heard about you. I'm Gladys Applebee," she said, extending her hand. "I think you started just after our office moved from City Hall. Well it's certainly a pleasure to finally meet you. What can I do for you boys today?"

Bobby moved closer and lowered his head.

"We need access to the archives to take a look at some records," he murmured in a low voice.

"Well you know the procedure, right?"

"Yeah I do," he answered, "but we ain't got time for all that. *Come on girl*, take care of us." He gave her a devious wink.

She thought about it for moment, tapping her pencil on the desk.

"All right," she said finally, motioning for us to bypass the others in line. "But don't be no stranger anymore ya hear...and feel free to bring your friend back with you." She winked at me as we made our way to the room behind her.

The room was filled with boxes, gray metal file cabinets and old microfilm readers. It seemed to be in complete disarray. I removed several boxes of folders from the top of an old desk to clear off some working space.

"Sounds like she's sweet on you Bobby."

"Who, Gladys? Naw, that old gal's a flirt that's all. We've known each other for years. Matter of fact, she was the Chief's secretary when I started in the department years ago. They never got along; they were both head strong, so he shipped her over to the County Clerk's Office. I'll bet she's been there at least ten years or more. Her husband died about eight years ago. God rest his soul." He pulled a chair over to the desk I had cleared off and sat down.

"I guess we both needed a shoulder to lean on. The bible says *Bear ye one another's burdens*. She's a sweet lady, just lonely that's all."

"Looks like she's sending you all the right signals," I teased, amused by the situation.

"Now I know there's a lot to be said for companionship. It feeds the soul they say, but I'm just not ready. To be honest, I don't know if I'll ever be again." Erleen's a hard act to follow," he said sadly. "By the way, what are we looking for?"

"Earl and Sue's marriage license."

"Why we looking for that?" he asked.

"It's gotta be here somewhere in all this clutter," I said, avoiding the question. "But where?"

He looked around the room. "Well your guess is as good as mine. Everything is so messy. We can make better time if you take that side of the room near the door. I'll start going through the file cabinets on this side. Between the two of us, maybe we can find the license."

"Sounds like a plan to me" I answered.

"And watch out for them spiders," he added.

"Spiders? You're kidding *right*?" I've hated spiders since I had a bad experience as a child.

"You city boys is scared of anything that crawls, ain't ya'll?" he laughed out loud.

I carefully moved a large box on the floor with my foot.

For the next hour he rummaged through file drawers while I opened boxes and microfilm cases. After about an hour we finally made some headway.

"Found the M's" he yelled from across the room. I dropped what I was doing and joined him, splitting the files between us.

"Here we go," he said, holding up a file after about twenty minutes of digging. We spread the documents across the top of the desk.

"Sue Ellen Rogers and Earl Howard McKenna, married January 5th, 1952," he read after adjusting his glasses.

"So they'd been married only ten years? How old did you say their daughter was when she disappeared?"

"Eighteen" he answered.

"So that would make her...twenty now" I said.

"Yeah and only ten when Sue Ellen and Earl were married," added Bobby.

"So Earl's her stepfather. Let's see if we can find the daughter's birth certificate. That should tell us who her father is. It's gotta be around here somewhere."

"Yeah, I just saw those files. They're over here," Bobby said, pointing to a row of old gray file cabinets he had previously searched. For the next hour we pulled birth records for everyone with the name of Catherine born in 1942, but came up empty handed.

"Maybe she was born in another county or state?"

"I don't think so, but I could be wrong," answered Bobby scratching his head. We started over, this time going through *every* birth record in the county for 1942, examining each record one by one. Luckily I hit the jackpot just as were reaching the end of the second go round.

"Well I'll be damned! We were looking for the wrong person."

"What you talking about?" Bobby asked curiously.

"Look at this." I gave him the birth certificate. He stared at it for a moment before his eyes widened as big as two silver dollars.

"Well I'll be a monkey's uncle. *Katherine Jane Wilson,* born to Sue Ellen Rogers and David Allen Wilson, August 18, 1942" We looked at each other - KJ. Her birth name was spelled with a K, not a C. Why it was changed? I removed the medallion from my pocket and took a look at the engraving. Maybe the person who gave her this medallion might also be connected in some way to her disappearance. At this point, who knows? I had a hunch, but decided to keep it to myself for the time being.

"You know anything about the father?" I asked.

"David Allen? Yeah. He works over at Atlas. He's in my bowling club, but I never knew this. Strange, in all the years I've known him, he never mentioned that."

"Atlas?"

"Yeah, Atlas Construction," he answered.

Sue Ellen had mentioned the name during questioning. She had overheard the name in Earl's argument with the Mayor on the phone the night he was killed.

"What's this Allen guy do there?"

"He's the finance manager."

"Maybe he's a suspect," I suggested.

"David Allen? Why would Sue Ellen try to protect *him* by confessing to the murder?" asked Bobby.

"Ex-husband protecting his battered ex-wife and mother of his child, perhaps? Sounds to me like a prime murder suspect, don't you think?" I placed the birth certificate back in its folder and under my arm.

"He just don't seem like the kinda guy that would do something like that," Bobby said thoughtfully.

"At this point we need to follow *every* lead. Maybe we should pay him a visit," I suggested, heading toward the door.

"Hey there young fella. Ain't you forgetting something?" Bobby asked, looking at the folder under my arm.

"Yeah. At which end of building *did we park*?" I asked.

"Lord have mercy on us!" he mumbled under his breath as he followed me out the door.

CHAPTER EIGHTEEN

"What do you know about the Atlas Construction Company?" I asked as we returned to the squad car to plot our next move.

"It's only the biggest construction company in the State of Georgia. Their headquarters are right here in Savannah. They won a contract from the City of Savannah to tear down parts of Park Hill about a year ago. From what I hear, they plan to build some pretty fancy homes on that land."

I'm not surprised. It was pattern that seemed to be taking hold in a lot of major cities across the country. After a mass exodus to the suburbs in the forties and fifties, the white middle class had begun to move *from* rural areas like Lakewood Estates *back* to the big city. In the process, they were reclaiming those areas forcing colored people out of those communities. They even had a fancy name for it – gentrification.

We were able to avoid the afternoon traffic by sticking to the back roads and made it over to the other side town just before five o'clock. I'd driven by the building several times but had never noticed the Atlas sign out front. By now the parking lot was starting to empty as the day shift began to leave. The heat rising from the black asphalt lot made the temperature feel more like a hundred degrees rather than the eighty-five degrees reported on the radio. Combined with the humidity, it made for a miserable afternoon. It had rarely ever felt this hot in New York.

We waited in the lobby after speaking with the receptionist, taking a moment to cool off while she did her best to find David Allen. She returned a few minutes later with a gentleman about fiftyish, dressed in a poorly tailored dark suit and white shirt carrying an armful of file folders.

"Well I'll be damn if it ain't Bobby Lee," he exclaimed, reaching out to shake his hand. "Sorry to keep you boys waiting. Man, it's been a long time. Where you been hiding?" You still staying in that old trailer?"

"I'm fine," Bobby answered. "I believe the last time I ran into you was at Tipton Haywood's funeral a few years back."

"Yeah you right. That was about four years ago," he answered. "Man, how time flies. You looking good, boy!"

"I've been blessed," said Bobby. "This here's my partner, Tyler Monroe. He's new in the department."

"Pleased to meet you,...Detective?" he asked, extending his hand.

"That's right. Detective Monroe," I answered, giving him a firm handshake.

"You don't sound like you're from around here," he said curiously.

"New York."

"New York? Man, you're a long way from home. What brings you down to this part of the country?" he asked.

"Just trying to get away from the hustle up north," I replied.

"So you must be a Yankees' fan. Think they'll take the series?" he asked.

"San Francisco's tough," I answered, "but we've got Mantle, Marris and Whitey. It'll be one hella series. It's one of the few things I do miss down here."

"We'll see. So what brings you boys over to this side of town?" he asked.

"Sorry for dropping in on you unannounced, but we're following up on a department matter. Is there somewhere we can talk in private?" Bobby inquired.

"Well sure, I… suppose so," he said, a little surprised. "We've got us a real nice meeting room right down here at the end of the hall," he indicated, pointing to his right. We followed Allen down the hall and into a large conference room.

"Make yourself comfortable," he said as we took a seat at a large circular table in the center of the wood-paneled conference room. "Can I get you boys something to drink?"

"Now that sounds mighty good to me. I'll take some ice water," responded Bobby, waving his handkerchief in front of his face to cool off.

"And you Detective?" he asked, pointing to a large bar on the left that appeared to be well stocked. I spotted a bottle of Simons Rum. That's stuff's twenty-five years old and undeniably as smooth as a woman's…

"Thanks for the offer," Bobby remarked, giving me a long stare, "but we're still on duty."

"Mind if I smoke, Mr. Allen?"

"Go ahead. Be my guest. I believe there's an ashtray around here somewhere." He picked up the phone at the end of the table and asked the receptionist to bring a pitcher of ice water. I lit a Marlboro and strolled around the room while we waited. On the wall hung portraits of the company's current and past presidents, all white, male and old.

"I think I know why you're here," he said, taking a seat directly across from us and shifting nervously.

"Me and Sue Ellen – that's the past. That's been over for a long, long time. We've both moved on. We both remarried. I mean, what else I can tell ya? As a matter of fact I," he stopped as the receptionist entered the room with a large picker of ice water.

"Is there anything else?"

"That'll be all for now. Thanks Maureen."

"When's the last time you talked to her?" I asked after the receptionist left the room, closing the door behind her.

"The last time? I guess it's been a few years now. Round about the time..." He paused for a moment before continuing, "Katherine disappeared. Before that, we hadn't talked in years.

It's unfortunate that something like that brings people back together ain't it"?

"I never knew she was your daughter," Bobby said regretfully, looking down at the table and nervously fumbling with his pen. "I guess I owe you an apology."

"Hell. I know it wasn't your fault Bobby. Sometimes I just believe things happen for a reason. But you know, deep down inside, I still believe she's okay. I know we'll see her again. Jesus said *all things are possible to him that believeth,*" David replied.

"Amen to that!" Bobby agreed.

"Do you know much about their relationship?" I asked, placing what was left of my cigarette in the ashtray.

"You mean Sue Ellen and Earl?"

"Yeah."

"Well...not much personally."

"Did you know he was physically abusive?"

"No I didn't," he murmured with a blank look on his face. "It's a damn good thing I *didn't* know about it," he said angrily. "I woulda..."

"Killed him perhaps?" I asked, using that question to draw out a possible motive.

"Now wait just a damn minute Mister! If you're trying to suggest for one minute that *I* had something to do with his murder you're barking up the wrong tree. Tell him Bobby. You know me better than that!"

"Look a here, I know this is hard for you D, but we got a hunch that maybe Sue Ellen acted in self-defense," Bobby suggested, attempting to calm him down.

"So, you think Sue Ellen is innocent?" he asked.

"Assuming it was a clear case of self-defense, then, yes," I answered.

He turned around, took a deep breath and exhaled.

"What I'm about to tell you doesn't leave this room. Understand?"

"You got my word," promised Bobby who turned and looked at me. I nodded in agreement. David got up and walked over to the window, looking out as he began to speak.

"I knew about the abuse," he admitted solemnly. "It started about a year after their marriage."

"How'd you find out?" I asked.

"She told me," he answered still looking out the window and not at us. He took another deep breath and exhaled.

"We carried on an affair for a while. We both knew it was wrong, but we couldn't help it. The sins of the flesh are powerful."

"Amen," Bobby agreed.

"She wasn't happy, but stayed in the marriage anyway."

"Why? " I asked.

"I guess you could say it was a...*marriage of convenience*."

"Meaning what?" I asked.

"Seems Earl McKenna had a bad habit of patronizing the bars on Mulberry Street late at night" he answered.

"Mulberry Street? Christ Almighty!" said Bobby, looking down and shaking his head.

"Meaning what?" I asked, unfamiliar with the area.

"Well, let's just say it's an area of the city patronized by men only," Bobby said. "Your get my drift?"

"Earl had big political aspirations," David Allen continued, "and he needed a *beard.* He was a good provider but he was one *insecure son of a bitch* – listening to Sue Ellen's phone calls, keeping tabs on her whereabouts. He knew something was going on behind his back and was afraid it might start rumors that could hurt his career. When our daughter disappeared, we stopped. The suffering drove us back to reality."

"What about Sue Ellen" I asked. What was she getting out of this arrangement?"

"Social status and wealth" he answered, and a better life for her daughter. She was one ambitious lady I'll tell ya."

"I can't believe I'm hearing this," said a shocked Bobby, shaking his head. "We've known each other for years. This just doesn't sound like you D. Why?"

"All I can say is, I'm sorry it happened," he admitted, finally turning around to face us.

"Where were *you* the night of the murder?" I asked.

"The church bowling league meets at Ten-Pin Lanes on Saturday nights. You can confirm that if you'd like."

"That won't be necessary, but I am interested in Earl's connection with Atlas. On the night of the murder, she overheard a phone conversation her husband had with the Mayor, who was upset about something to do with Atlas. Any idea what they might have been talking about?"

He sat back down at the table, putting his head down between his hands. "Atlas has been under investigation by DA's office for about a year now. Apparently there are some concerns about how the deal we closed with the city to tear down parts of Park Hill was awarded."

"What kind of concerns?" Bobby asked.

"Payoffs, but that's just hearsay. I don't know nothing about it and you didn't hear any of this from me, okay?" he sputtered, avoiding eye contact with both of us.

"And I assume that deal went through the Mayor's office?" I asked.

"That's correct," David Earl confirmed.

"So it's possible the argument McKenna had with the Mayor the night of the murder may have had something to do with the investigation of Atlas?"

"Possibly," he answered. It was no wonder the Mayor and the Chief were in a hurry to close this case.

"Look, I don't mean to cut you guys short, but I really need to get back to work," he said. "But I'd be more than happy to help in any way, if you think it'll clear Sue Ellen's name."

"I understand. Just one more question if you don't mind." I reached into my pocket, removed the medallion and handed it to him. "This was found at the murder scene. Any idea who might have given this to your daughter?" He studied the medallion for a moment, reading the inscription on the back before returning it.

"No idea" he answered.

Bobby got up from the table and gave him a hug. "Thanks for taking the time to speak with us," he said. "I know you must be carrying a lot of pain inside. You know where to find me if you ever need someone to talk to."

David Allen's admissions had stunned us both. Neither one of us knew what to make of them, or how they factored into the case. He seemed sincere about his love for Sue Ellen and he certainly had a motive, but he just didn't fit the profile of a jealous lover who might commit a murder. Hopefully my gut feeling would turn out to be correct. Also just the sheer mention of KJ sent him into a deeply depressed state, so there was no use in pursuing that angle…at least not now. It appears Atlas had somehow finagled the Park Hill construction contract with the Mayor, leading to an investigation.

CHAPTER NINETEEN

It was a cool summer morning, unusual for this time of year. Perhaps a sign of an early fall? After such a brutal summer, I certainly hoped so. The attendant at the entrance to the gravesites directed me to the visitor's lot. I parked before making my way across the dew covered manicured grounds. To my surprise, there were quite a few people around at this hour of the morning, all dressed in black. Using the map I'd received from the person on duty at the entrance, I eventually located the freshly prepared plot. It was exquisitely decorated with fresh arrangements of red and white roses and the marble tombstone was correctly engraved with the dates 1900 – 1962 as requested. I removed my hat and sat down on the cold, damp earth. Memories of my childhood flashed before me. I knew this day would eventually come; I just wasn't prepared for it to come this soon. Unfortunately life operates on its own schedule.

"Ain't doing you no good sitting on that cold hard ground," a voice from behind me warned. "They got chairs if you want to sit down you know. Ain't no use in messing up that nice suit of yours."

"I'm fine," I answered, still staring at the tombstone in front of me.

"I expected as much. Hard headed just like your daddy."

I spun around abruptly to find an older lady wearing a white dress and a white wide brim hat. She had the same auburn hair as Martha, but a much darker complexion.

"Oh my lord, you look just like him," she said quietly, with a look somewhere between joy and disbelief. "I bet you don't remember me do you? You was just a little boy bout' this high when I left New York" she said smiling, holding both hands straight out in front of her. I didn't recognize the face and I'm certain I had never met her before.

"As kids, your mother and I left the South and went up north looking for a better life. Well, a lifetime later, here we are again," she said with a chuckle…"back where we started." She shook her head. "Life's strange ain't it?" I was still confused as to who she was.

"Oh I'm sorry," she said, sensing my confusion. "I'm your Aunt Doriece, Martha's sister." Sister? That's strange. She never mentioned a sister before. That certainly explained the resemblance.

"How did you know…?"

"I never went back," she interjected before I could finish my question, "but I always stayed in touch with the family. I knew she was down here. I also heard that you finally talked to your daddy after all these years."

"Can we leave him out of this?"

She stared at me for a moment before taking off her shoes and gathering her dress in order to sit down on the damp ground next to me.

"It's about time you let that go Boy. Why can't you just forgive him?"

"It'll be a cold day in Hell when that happens."

"The Heavenly Father teaches us that forgiveness is a virtue," Aunt Doriece challenged.

Having to listen to Bobby day in and day out about the virtues of God was enough. Now this? I just couldn't seem to get away from these Bible thumping fanatics.

"So why does this God you speak of take the life of innocent people while low life scum roam the streets? Explain that, because it makes absolutely no sense to me."

"I believe God makes us experience pain so that we will appreciate the joys in life. Sounds strange, don't it? You'd think it be the other way around now wouldn't you?"

She paused for a moment and placed her hand on mine. "I know you never got over the death of your little brother. Died in your arms didn't he?" she asked quietly. "You gotta stop blaming yourself. It wasn't your fault. It was his time son but he's walking with the Lord now. Both he and his Momma are in a better place."

"My brother and I were raised in the church and we followed the words of the Bible. I believed there was a God but no matter how hard we prayed, life never got any better for us. We went to church looking for answers but all we ever got was a lot of empty rhetoric between the passing of offering plates. So go ahead and believe in your God if that's what you need to get through life. I choose not to," I said.

She smiled and looked out over the vast landscape, while removing her hat and placing it on the ground between us. "Oh he's real, believe me," she insisted softly with a big smile, "but you got a lotta pain deep inside you Son that's turned into anger. The only way to deal with that pain is through forgiveness. You understand what I'm saying? That needs to start with your father. I can tell you still carrying that around like a giant weight on your shoulders but I'll say it again, at some point you need to let that go. Now I'll be the first to admit that he did wrong by you and Martha and there ain't no excuse for that, but he *tried* to make it up to you."

"Bullshit!"

"Now you just wait a minute Boy," she snapped. "When you was growing up, how do you think you got in them good schools uptown? You think you got in *just because they thought you was white*?" When you went to that college up north they said you had a scholarship *didn't they*? You *never* paid a cent did you? And you got in the Police Academy *awful easy* even with *yo low score*s didn't you?" She paused for a moment before continuing. "Don't you understand boy? *Your* daddy was *always* there in the background looking out for you. *You just didn't know it.*"

I could feel the urge for a drink right about now. Was it actually true?

"You were a just a baby then…too young to understand" she said sadly while looking out across the field. "He was running for Mayor back then, just after you was born. If the town had found out that he'd gotten "the help" pregnant, his career would have been finished before it ever got started. Look at me Boy!" she said sternly. "Can't you understand that he never *wanted to,* but he *had* to cut his ties with you and Martha, yet you were always his son and he never stopped loving you and your brother?"

"Why didn't he just…tell me all this?" I asked, hurting and still skeptical.

"Maybe he just didn't know *how.*"

I thought about it for a moment. The promotions, the deal with the Feds…it had been *all too easy.* I had always wondered…of all the eligible candidates in the Bronx precinct, why me? Now it was all starting to make sense.

"But did I *really* deserve all of the special treatment; did I earn it?"

"Of course you did Son," she said proudly. "And yo momma made sure everybody knew it, too" she said with a big grin. "Child, that woman loved you like nobody's business."

"I'll miss her," I said sadly.

"Oh I reckon you'll see her again one day," she responded.

"Think so?"

"Oh I know so," she answered softly, her face changing to a smile. "As God is my witness."

"I'd like to be alone with her if you don't mind?" I asked, finally getting up from the cold hard ground.

"Well if you ever need to talk, I'm here for you," she offered. "Your momma always said that when it comes to faith, it's not what you *think*, it's what you *feel*. The mind may deceive, but the *heart never lies*. As long as you remember that, you'll be all right" she assured me, getting up and giving me a big hug.

"How will I…"

"Don't worry," she interrupted before I could finish. "I'll find *you*. What's meant to be will always find its way. Remember that," she answered with a mysterious grin as she turned to walk away. Where had I heard that before?

I remained at the gravesite for a few minutes longer before saying my final goodbye to my mother. In a strange way I felt both sadness and relief-- I'm not sure why. After a few words, I arranged the flowers neatly at the base of her gravestone. The humidity was rising and the morning dew had all but disappeared. I looked in both directions; Aunt Doriece was nowhere in sight - gone just that quick, just like the old blind man in the Greyhound station.

"Hey buddy," yelled the parking attendant, waving his hand from across the way to catch my attention. "Hey there. You okay Son?"

"Yeah, I think so," I answered slowly, still in a daze from all I had just learned. He put down a large shovel and walked over to me while brushing his overalls that were completely covered with dirt.

"Now I know this is a real hard time for you and your loved ones, but you can take comfort in the fact that they're at peace with our Lord in Heaven. You'll be okay. It happens to everyone."

"What are you talking about? What happens?" I asked.

"Well" he answered, looking down and hesitating before continuing, "I saw you over there at that gravesite. Looks like you was carrying on a conversation," he paused…"with yourself."

"Myself? What about the lady who..."

"Lady? What lady?" he asked. "Like I said, it happens," he continued, lightly patting me on the shoulder. "We all deal with grief in different ways, but time heals all pains. If you looking for your car, it's right down that path to your right."

I walked back to the squad car and got in, emotionally somewhere between shock and denial. Was she real or was it just my imagination? I removed a small silver flask hidden under the seat. It was a fragile moment; probably similar to the one junkies have just before shoving that needle in their vein. Hands shaking, I slowly raised it to my lips. Two weeks on the wagon was about to come to an end. The sweet aroma of its contents escaped the bottle as I slowly removed the top. JD was calling the shots and I was a blind follower. Just before taking that frightening step; however, my conscience kicked in and I tossed it out the window. I grabbed the steering wheel tightly with both hands, placed my head in the center of it and began to quietly cry.

Her light complexion and long reddish brown hair were features you'd expect from someone of European descent rather than from those of freed slaves. It allowed her to straddle two separate societies, one of which she eventually decided to abandon forever. The old folks called it *passing* – posing as a white person in order to escape the prejudice that colored folks suffered in this country. It was common practice for those of us who could cross over the color line but in most cases it meant leaving behind both family *and* community forever. It was a heavy, costly sacrifice to pay for a better life. Was it worth the price?

As a child I never understood why the two of us constantly moved from town to town or why she taught me to say "Yes Ma'am" instead of "yes 'am." I grew up never having the opportunity to be spoiled by grandparents or hear them reminiscence about the "good old days" or the way things used to be. She worked a variety of jobs, sometimes two or three at a time, leaving me home alone at night with a stack of books I was forced to read over and over. Growing up and never having any real friends made it difficult for me to build relationships as an adult.

It was not until my younger brother died that we returned to the place she had called home and I found out the real truth about who I really was. At the funeral I finally met cousins, uncles, and aunts I'd never met before – all of whom to my surprise were colored. I was both angry and confused.

At the age of fifteen, how could I process that? I had become accustomed to a life where acceptance in society was defined by skin color and social status. I considered myself privileged and looked down upon the less fortunate and the less educated Negroes. Now shockingly, I found myself on *their* side of the color line!

As a young woman, my mother had made the decision to forsake the rest of her family and live a false life. As I grew older I would finally realize that this incredible sacrifice *was for me.* Attending the better schools, wearing the better clothes and traveling the world were all possible because of my skin color. Eventually at some point in my life, I too would also have to choose. The guilt became a tremendous burden for me. In many ways, I hated *both* sides of who I was. Eventually alcohol became the crutch I relied on to suppress both my guilt and my demons.

CHAPTER TWENTY

"Let's go over this one more time," he repeated, reaching over to turn off the radio to get my attention. I took one last drag and flipped what was left of my cigarette out the passenger side window.

"Again? How many times do we have to do this?"

"Until we get it right. We can't afford no mistakes. You understand me?" Bobby insisted.

"Last time?" I asked.

"Last time," he promised.

I exhaled and slumped down in my seat, feeling like a first grader practicing for the big school play.

"Go to the intersection of Alameda and 33rd. Park and wait for an unmarked car to pull up behind me. Someone will get out and hand me a briefcase through the open car window."

"You know the line?" he asked.

"Yeah."

"Then what?" he demanded.

"Exit the car. Walk down 33rd towards Remington. Drop the briefcase in a blue garbage can behind the old Hilltop Barber Shop.

And make sure *nobody* sees you do it!" he added.

"Right. Then what?" I asked.

"Then you get the hell outta there. Got that?" he answered, giving me a long hard stare. "Don't screw this up, ya hear me?"

He opened the door and got out, disappearing quickly into the darkness.

I made a brief detour at the gas station to pick up a pack of Marlboros and a grape soda before driving to the drop off spot. It was another hot and humid night. Too hot, in fact to be playing delivery boy for a money drop, but the Feds needed to know who the players were in this racket. It was my ticket out of this nightmare.

At eleven that night the streets were empty, not even a bum or prostitute. As planned, I pulled over and parked on 33rd, just shy of Alameda. To kill time I switched on the radio only to be reminded that the local stations all go off at sundown. Desperate for a distraction, I went up and down the radio dial listening for a signal. Not surprised the only thing I could find at this hour was a country western station. It was either that or nothing at all. Bored, I took out the medallion and studied the inscription again. *I will always love you, KJ.* Was it from KJ confessing her love *for someone,* or was it from someone to KJ, confessing love for her?

Luckily my musings were cut short as I noticed a vehicle in my rear view mirror slowly pulling up behind me. The lights went off just as it stopped within a few feet of my rear end. Without streetlights it was next to impossible to see who it was. After several minutes the car door opened and a figure emerged. I slowly slid my right hand under my jacket and unfastened the strap holding my pistol - just in case. As he got closer, I spotted a briefcase in his left hand. His right hand was in his pocket. He walked up to the window and stood silently for a second before speaking.

"Sure is cold out here tonight" he said while shining a flashlight in my face making it impossible to see him.

"It's always cold in the North Pole," I replied nervously. Satisfied, he passed a brown leather briefcase through the window. It was the same leather briefcase Bobby had taken from the back room of his trailer a few days ago. Without saying another word, he quickly turned around and walked back to the car behind me, then drove off.

Content that he was gone and no one else was around, I opened the brief case. Inside were neatly stacked bundles of hundred dollar bills – possibly five to ten thousand dollars in cash, by my estimate. On impulse, some folks might take the money, head across the border into Mexico, change their names and live a luxurious life. I'll admit, it *was* tempting, but eventually the Feds or the mob would find me. Either way it wouldn't be a happy ending.

Sticking to the script, I walked down 33rd towards Remington with the briefcase firmly tucked under my arm. The next and final stop was the Hilltop Barber Shop. The Hilltop was a "colored only" establishment. It was a small storefront with a large front window that allowed customers to see how busy it was inside before deciding to go in. From what I hear, it was the best seventy-five cent hair cut in town. Levi was rumored to be a "principal investor" in the business, which meant he probably used it to funnel money from his prostitution ring and drug racketeering.

As rehearsed, I walked to the end of the block and down a small alley leading to the back of the building. However *two* large trashcans had been placed at the back door of the building instead of one. The briefcase was to be placed inside the blue trashcan. But because of the enduring curse of colorblindness, I had no idea which one was blue.

Frustrated, I tried looking at both cans from different angles to distinguish the color as best as I could. My intuition leaned towards the one on the left. Hopefully that was the correct one. At this point I didn't give a damn. I just wanted to finish the drop off and get the hell outta this part of town. Unfortunately my fears became reality as I noticed several figures approaching from the other side of the building. It was almost as if they had appeared out of nowhere. I got a bad feeling in my stomach.

"What business you got around here this time of night white boy?" asked a short figure wearing a black hooded mask with holes cut out at the eyes. I didn't answer.

"What's the matter? Can't you hear white boy?"

He wore an oversized white tee shirt and a pair of black high top sneakers. He stood about all of four feet tall. Standing behind him were four larger gang members wearing similar masks. From his voice I guessed he couldn't be more that fourteen.

I clutched the briefcase under my arm tightly without answering as they surrounded me. A bad night was about to get worse. One of the other four pulled out the longest switchblade I'd ever seen. "Maybe we ought to carve his honky ass up, just like they did little Willie." He flipped the blade open and placed it between my legs a few inches shy of the family jewels. "Crackers killed him for nothing! He was just a kid."

He was talking about the murder of a nine-year old boy found hanging from a tree about a year ago in Mississippi. A federal inquiry was conducted but no perpetrators were ever caught or prosecuted, a real travesty of justice.

"What you wanna' do wit this cracker?" he asked the others.

"Let's give him a haircut," said one. He took the switchblade from down below and put it behind my right ear. "When I finish with 'em, his own momma won't recognize him. How you like it white boy? Close on the sides and tight in the back?" They all laughed.

Luckily my pistol was in its holster under the same arm holding the briefcase. I'd never shot a kid before and I really didn't want any of these kids to be the first, but if it were a matter of life and death…

"I got a better idea," said another. He appeared to be a little older, judging from his size and the sound of his voice, maybe the leader. He motioned for the kid on my left to step forward.

"If you wanna roll with us, YOU gotta take care of business," he explained to his companion. He placed the switchblade in this kid's hand. "Cut his ass up!" he ordered. I guess this was his initiation. His uneasiness confirmed that. I could also smell alcohol on his breath.

"This cracker got some money," the one charged to cut me up said to the others after staring me down for a minute. "Check out them clothes he got on. Let's take this punk's clothes *and* his money," he suggested, "and then I'll cut his ass up!"

"I got first on them bad ass shoes," said another.

"What the hell is wrong with y'all? We don't need no goddamn clothes or no goddamn shoes," yelled the apparent leader, shoving the one holding the switchblade to the side.

If they were older I'd drop all five without a second thought. It would clearly be a case of self-defense but they were just kids, looking for trouble. Unfortunately the media would never see it that way. Reluctantly I reached down and unbuttoned my coat, holding on tightly to the briefcase with the other hand. I was still hoping to avoid the situation turning ugly.

"Hold on. I got this," said another gang member, who had up to this point remained silent. "Let me have his cracker ass." He took the blade from the kid and placed it under my chin and across the front of my throat. He leaned forward, almost eye-to-eye.

"What the hell you doing down here?" he whispered. That voice belonged to Sonny Boy. I breathed a brief sigh of relief but no way was I going to reveal the fact that I had over ten grand of the mob's money under my arm.

"I know you ain't lost. So why you down here?" he whispered, then said, louder, "I'll bet you trying to score some smack, ain't ya?" I took the bait.

"Yeah. I heard this is the place. You got the hookup?"

"Depends. How much green you got in yo pocket?" I reached down with my free hand and pulled out two crisp one hundred dollar bills that I had taken out of the briefcase back in the car as my "drop off " fee. Easy come easy go. His eyes lit up.

"There's more where that came from, if you guys want to do a little business on a regular basis," I added. He looked around at the others before answering.

"All right," he said loudly, placing the blade down by his side. "Wait right here and we'll be right back wit the smack." He stuffed the money in his back pocket before stepping closer, nose-to-nose.

"We even white boy?" he whispered.

"Yeah," I answered. "We even."

He stepped back and winked before taking off running with the others close behind, all laughing as they headed down the alley and up the street. I could hear one of them yell "stupid cracker" as they disappeared into the darkness.

I stood there numb for a few minutes to make sure they were finally gone before placing the leather briefcase in one of the trashcans. I didn't give a damn if it was the right one or not. The only thing on my mind at the moment was getting back to the car and getting the hell out of this part of town. A drink was definitely somewhere in that plan too.

CHAPTER TWENTY-ONE

I double parked next to a white Cadillac, removed my badge from my pocket and placed it inside the front window to avoid getting towed. After putting my revolver under the seat I quickly made my way to the main entrance. Once inside, I spotted Bobby near Lane 13.

"Well it's about time," he whispered with a concerned look as I sat down next to him. "So…how did it go?"

"All done," I answered.

"Thank God," he breathed. "Thank God."

"Where's David Allen?" I asked, changing the subject.

"He's around here somewhere. I think he went to grab a beer," Bobby replied.

"That sounds good. I could use one too."

"From the looks of things I think you've already had your share for tonight. I can smell it on you a mile away," he said, disgusted.

I had stopped at a liquor store on the way over to calm my nerves. Considering what I'd been through tonight I was due a stiff one, maybe two.

"I'm not on duty so what I do *on my tim*e is *my business* and I'm getting damn tired of you telling me what I…"

"I see you finally made it," interrupted David Allen, walking up from behind and patting me on the back. He wore an orange shirt with the words FIRST BAPTIST BOWLING CLUB embroidered across the front.

"Looks like they're about to shut down the lanes but the bar is open until eleven. We can talk there. Give us a minute to turn in our shoes and we'll meet you there."

"Sounds like a plan," I answered, heading in the direction of the front entrance.

"Hey," yelled David Allen. "It's that way," he pointed in the other direction.

I was definitely a little tipsy at this point.

The "bar" was a small dimly lit area with no more than ten tables. It was virtually empty. A bartender made small talk at the bar with a few customers while pouring shots. I decided to take a table in the back next to the jukebox. After a few minutes a waitress stopped at the table to take my order.

"What ya having honey?" she asked. She was cute, but very young.

"JD on the rocks…and hold the rocks, okay?"

"Sure thing, you got it baby," she answered heading back to bar just as Bobby and David Allen entered and sat down.

"You having anything to drink, David?" I asked.

"I'm okay, thanks," he answered. "Believe me, I've had my share tonight."

"It's getting late. We don't want to hold you up too long, so what were you able to find out?" Bobby asked.

"First of all, you never heard any of this from me, got that? I could lose my job." We both nodded. He looked around the room before continuing.

"I was able to take a look at the books for the Park Hill project just as you had asked. Those books stay locked up in my boss's office but I have a key to the safe. I just hope like hell nobody saw me."

"How'd you get the key?" Bobby asked.

"I took over the department temporarily when the old finance director left so I had the key to that safe. When the new guy was hired I had a copy made in case he ever lost the original. I never figured I'd be using it for something like this," he whispered, nervously looking around the bar before continuing.

"I found the bids for the project. There were three submittals. Atlas was the lowest bidder. They were at least a *half million below* the other two bids. I know that sounds odd, but that's not the big revelation," he said, lowering his voice even more.

"To date there's been twelve change orders on the contract, all approved by the Mayor's office. Those change orders alone account for roughly 1.2 million dollars."

"So they came in low to get the contract?" I asked.

"Yeah, and they're making it all back and more on the changes."

"But isn't that what they all do?" asked Bobby.

"Yeah that's how it's done all right, but if you look at each change order you'll see they're all for the same work." We sat there staring at each other trying to make sense of what he had just said.

"How in the hell can you turn in the same change order twelve times?"

"I don't know," he conceded shaking his head, "but probably some clerk in the Mayor's office discovered what was happening and went to the DA's office."

"So you think that's how Earl got involved?" I asked.

"Probably."

"So that might suggest Atlas had Earl murdered to cover up the scam." Bobby said.

"I don't think so," he answered. "Atlas might be stealing money, but they're not murderers."

"Are you sure about that?" I asked.

"I been at this company for twenty-two years next December. I just don't believe it's something Atlas would get involved in. As far as Earl's murder is concerned, I think you're barking up the wrong tree with this."

"Maybe he's right," admitted Bobby.

I guess that made sense. Even with Earl's murder, someone else in the DA's office would simply pick up the pieces and continue the investigation. His death would focus *more* attention, if anything, on his investigation of Atlas. It would have been a dumb move for Atlas to have killed him.

"Well, we can't talk to anyone in the DA's office because we're not supposed to be involved in this case" said Bobby.

"So we're back to square one," I said.

"JB, no rocks," said the young waitress, holding a shot glass.

"It's late and I gotta get home," said David Allen. "Enjoy your drink."

"It's way past my bedtime too" said Bobby. "You gonna be all right Youngblood?"

"Yeah."

"You *sure*?" he asked, looking straight into my no doubt bloodshot eyes.

"I'm fine." I stood up slowly to regain my composure and reached out to shake David Earl's hand. "I appreciate all the help you provided, really. Thanks man."

"I don't mind at all as long as it helps Sue Ellen clear her name. Deep down in my heart I know she didn't have anything to do with this. I just wish I could prove it. If you need anything else from me, just let me know."

"Thanks," said Bobby, giving him a hug. "See ya at church on Sunday."

"God willing," he answered smiling. With David Allen heading for the door, Bobby turned his attention to me.

"Look at you boy. You a holy mess. You can hardly stand up straight. I'm driving you home, so don't even try to argue with me all right? We can come back and pick up the other car tomorrow."

"I told you I'm okay!" I answered, slurring my words slightly.

"I don't care what you say. You ain't driving in that condition. You'll kill your fool self. I'll go get the car and pull it around front. Meet me at the door in a couple of minutes." He disappeared as I sat back down to keep from passing out.

I gulped down what remained of my drink, then slammed the glass on the table, upside down, victorious. It brought back memories of my days at the academy when we all went out on Friday night to blow off steam. I missed those days.

"We'll be closing up in about ten minutes. Will you be needing anything else honey?" asked the waitress.

"I'm fine thanks." My head felt as if it were about to split in two.

"Well you have a good night," she replied, winking at me before heading back to the bar.

I picked up the check and suddenly realized I had given every dollar I had to Sonny Boy earlier tonight. Guess I'll have to slip out. At the bottom of the check I noticed a handwritten phone number…EL6-3893. Flattering, but I already had someone to go home to and that someone was going to be *pretty pissed* tonight.

CHAPTER TWENTY-TWO

"Well it's about damn time. Most of us start at seven o'clock around here or haven't you noticed?"

"Sorry Chief," I replied. "Long night."

"You sound like a damn broken record," he shot back. "In my office right now goddamnit!" That didn't sound good. I put down my oversized cup of black coffee, pushed back my old squeaky wooden desk chair and proceeded to the Chief's office as ordered.

"Baby's about to get spanked," gloated Pete, smiling as I walked by.

"Yeah, Wonder Boy about to get his ass kicked," added Andy. I wasn't sure what this was all about, but judging from their apparent joy, I could tell it wasn't going to be a pleasant experience.

"Sit down and shut the door," the chief ordered, leaning forward in his chair. He gave us a long stare. That alone was a bad sign. I complied and sat down next to a very nervous Bobby.

"What in the hell have you two been up to lately?" he asked emphatically. "I'm getting complaints from all over town about the two of you's sticking your noses into McKenna's murder investigation. I got niggers running through Long's, complaints from Greyhound, reports of you questioning citizens without their consent…and this!" he said. "What the hell is this?" he asked, holding up last night's bar bill with the words I.O.U. written on it.

"Ah, I can explain that Chief," I offered.

"Shut the hell up!" he yelled. "You don't speak until I tell you to. Now both of you listen to me. Have you heard that this case is closed?" he asked, pounding on his desk.

"But you see, Chief…"

"Yes, I *see* very well thank you. Read my damn lips…*this case is closed!*" he said, emphasizing each word slowly. "Is that too difficult for you two idiots to understand? And I'm surprised at *you.* You been at this longer than anybody here Bobby. You *know* better than that. As for you Mr. Monroe, is that the way you big city cops conduct business? Somebody tell me what the hell is going on and tell me *right now.*" We both sat there silently waiting for the other to speak first.

"We think there may be a connection between Earl's murder and his daughter's disappearance," I responded, finally breaking the silence.

"What did you say?" he asked, leaning forward.

"We think there's a connection to the murder."

He leaned back in his chair looking confused. "Well this better be good. Go on. Tell me what you got."

"We've got reason to believe there was someone else in the house the night of the murder."

"Based on?" he asked.

I reached into my coat pocket and pulled out the medallion. "This," I answered, reaching over to hand him the piece. "Take a look at the inscription on the back," I suggested.

He looked at it for a moment, still confused. "So who in the hell is KJ and what's the connection?"

"We believe it's the daughter Catherine Jane but Catherine spelled with a K, not a C. Her birth records confirm the spelling with a K."

"So why did she change it to a C?" he asked.

"We don't know," I answered.

"Okay, so now we know how she spells her name. Big deal," he said sarcastically. "You two expecting a medal for that? What's that got to do with her disappearance?"

"We found it in the house upstairs, on the floor in front of the master bedroom where Earl was found."

"So what? It could have been there for days, weeks, or even months," the chief shot back.

"We think whoever killed Earl may have dropped the medallion," I answered.

"That's all fine and dandy, but Sue Ellen confessed to the crime. What would be this other person's motivation anyway?" he asked. Bobby and I both looked at each other. We didn't have an answer for that.

"So you think the person who owns this medallion murdered McKenna *and* has something to do with this girl's disappearance?" he asked after waiting in vain for the answer.

"We don't know," answered Bobby, looking down at the floor. The Chief looked at both sides of the medallion again.

"Well, it looks pretty common to me. Why don't you just visit all the local jewelers to see if anyone recognizes it?"

Bobby and I glanced at each other, embarrassed. "That's a real good idea Chief," I answered. "We hadn't thought of that."

"Well that's why I'm the goddamn Chief here," he said, rolling his eyes. "Now let's set the record straight, okay? If you think you got something that might help us find Catherine, then by all means pursue it. But I haven't heard anything you've said so far to make me believe there's a connection to the murder. Got that?"

We nodded in agreement.

"Now get the hell out of my damn office."

CHAPTER TWENTY-THREE

"I been telling you all along, this was a bad idea from the git go."

"You been telling *me*?" I shouted. He put his finger to his lips, reminding me that even thought we were standing out in the hall we were still in hearing range of our two adversaries.

"You were the one that wanted closure on the case and I agreed to help you, remember?" I whispered.

"Well, we did find the medallion right? Don't that mean anything to you?" he asked. "And we both know Sue Ellen is lying. We can't just let that drop without finding out what really happened, right?" I took a deep breath to calm down.

"You're right. I didn't mean to yell at you. I'm sorry."

"Don't worry about it. He did say we could still investigate the medallion."

"Yeah, but what if we find a connection to David?" I asked.

"Then we do the right thing," he answered.

The Chief had hit on a brilliant idea when he suggested we visit all the local jewelers to see if any of them recognized the medallion. After all, *someone* had engraved it and sold it to the person we were looking for. My initial guess would be the kid Catherine had dated and broken up with. I pulled out my spiral pad to scan my notes. Clyde was his name.

"Do you know a Clyde…don't have a last name?" I asked flipping through my pages as we walked down Reed Boulevard towards the downtown business district.

"Clyde Dwyer. Oh yeah, I know 'em…a real hell raiser, barely made it through high school," Bobby replied.

"Really?"

Bobby continued, "I arrested him a couple of times. His parents were good friends with the Chief, so he never spent a night in a cell. I guess that's what money will do for you."

"Any connection to the disappearance?"

"No. He was the first person we talked to during the investigation being that they were dating at the time."

"And?"

"He checked out clean. He was outta town the week she disappeared."

"Where?" I asked.

"Football recruiting trip down at the University of Alabama. I talked to the coach. The kid never left campus during that time."

I drew a line through his name in my spiral pad and put it back in my pocket.

"It might be a whole lot faster if we split up," Bobby suggested as we stopped at the corner of Reed and Columbus. "Reveno's is two blocks down on the left. If you go another block down you'll see Silverman's on the other side of the street. I'll check out a couple of pawn shops on this end and meet you back at the luncheonette in an hour."

"And how can I help you today sir?" asked a gentleman as I entered Reveno's. It was a small shop with watches, rings, and gold necklaces neatly laid out in display cases pushed up against the wall.

"You folks sell medallions?" I asked.

"We most certainly do. Right this way sir," he said, directing me to a glass display case in the rear of the store.

"Looking for anything specific?"

"Yeah, ever seen this before?" I asked, handing him the medallion. He looked at it, flipping it from side to side.

"Can't say that I have, but I can sell it for you on consignment if you're looking to unload it. We can easily get at least a hundred dollars for this from some sucker."

I pulled out my badge and put it on top of the display case. His eyes doubled in size. I loved doing that.

"Just kidding Officer. This here's quality grade silver," he said. "We don't sell this type of stuff. You might try across the street," he suggested, pointing to Silverman's on the corner.

"Thanks." I put the medallion back in my pocket and picked up my badge.

"Any time Detective. Any time at all."

I waited for the light to change and walked across the street to Silverman's. Unlike Reveno's, this shop appeared to be a much newer and classier place. Once inside, an older woman approached me from behind a counter.

"What can I do for you today, sir?" she asked with a pleasant smile. I pulled out my badge and cut right to the chase.

"Ever seen this before," I asked, handing her the medallion. She studied the picture on the front for a moment before turning it over to look at the engraving. She smiled.

"Yes I have," she answered.

"Are you sure?" I asked, not believing what I had just heard.

"We don't sell anything of this quality, but we did do the engraving. I remember it well."

"Are you sure?" I asked.

"Of course I am. This is a V-point cut. I did the engraving myself."

"Can you describe the person who had the engraving done?" I asked nervously. She looked at the medallion again.

"I'm sorry, but I don't really recall. I've done some many of these."

"Here's my card and phone number in case you remember. It's very important. Can I get your card and number in case I have any more questions?" She removed one from behind the counter and gave it to me. I placed it in my pocket along with the medallion and headed for the door.

"Detective…Detective. Just a minute!" she yelled, rushing toward me as I opened to door to leave.

"Now that I've had a moment to think about it, I believe it was a young colored boy."

"A young colored boy? You *sure*?" I asked. "This is *very* important."

"Yes. It's coming back to me now. As I recall he didn't have enough money for the engraving, but I did it anyway. He seemed like such a nice boy and I could tell he was really in love."

"What do mean by that?"

"I sell these types of things here every day. I can tell from the look in their eyes that it's real love, and this was real love. You ever been in love?" she asked, sensing my skepticism.

"My personal business is not the issue here Madam. Are you're sure it was a young colored boy?" I asked her again.

"Yes, I'm sure."

CHAPTER TWENTY-FOUR

I headed straight for our favorite spot in the back, walking directly past Danita without a word. Bobby was already there and as usual, chowing down on his favorite desert.

I sat down, pulling the chair up close to the table. He could tell something was wrong by the look on my face. I took out a cigarette and nervously lit it.

"Silverman's" I said. "Silverman's did the engraving." his pie-filled mouth dropped wide open. He put his fork down on the table.

"Well I'll be. Who was it?"

"Sonny Boy," I whispered, still in a state of shock.

"Sonny? You sure? That don't make no sense to me," he said, rejecting that possibility. I moved closer and lowered my voice even more.

"Yes it does. Clyde cheated on Catherine with her best friend..."

"...and she promised she'd get back at him," he finished my thought, realizing the obvious. "Good Lord almighty." His face turned red and his eyebrows arched in anger. After all this was the South where interracial dating was still frowned upon.

"More than likely it was just revenge for her, but this kid was obviously in love," I said.

"All right. So what's that got to do with her disappearance?" he asked.

"Who knows" I answered. "We need to have a little talk with Sonny Boy. At least we know where we can find him."

"Check please."

CHAPTER TWENTY-FIVE

"Yeah?" the voice behind the slider said. I held up my badge. "We're here to see Levi."

We followed the now familiar doorman to the main ballroom where Levi sat at the bar. He was engaged in conversation with a sexy young lady and puffing on his signature Cuban cigar.

"Well I'll be damn, if it ain't the boys from downtown. You boys a little early this week ain't ya?" He placed his cigar in large ashtray and took a sip of his martini.

"Where can we find Sonny Boy," I asked, ignoring his comment.

He put down his drink and stared at me for a moment. "Light blue tie on top of a pink shirt. I like that. You got taste Detective" he said. "Remind me to pick up that combination Bo."

"Yes sir Mr. Levi," answered Bo.

"So ya'll looking for that nigger too? Well I hope to God you find him before I do, cause if I find him, I'm going cut his throat." Bobby and I looked at each other, confused.

"He did a pick up for me last night but I ain't seen or heard from him. I know that nigger took off with my damn money," he said. "Gotta be at least a grand or more."

"This here's a small town" said Bobby. "He won't get very far."

"That's what you think" he said. "Word on the street is he was seen at the bus station last night, probably headed up North."

Goddamnit. I shot a quick glance at Bobby. We were both probably thinking the same thing - if that's true, he's gone for good. We had finally gotten a lead on Catherine's disappearance and it had suddenly fallen apart.

"Atlanta, New York, Chicago, it don't matter, I'll find his ass," said Levi, taking a long, slow sip of his martini. "It's just a matter of time." He turned to the young lady sitting next to him.

"Go on upstairs and wait for me while I take care of some business, baby," he said with a wink. Two of his henchmen followed her.

"Drink?" Levi offered, holding up his martini and looking directly at me. "It's mighty hot outside. Oh damn…I forgot you boys is on duty. Well, cheers." He took another sip and placed his glass back on the bar, motioning for us to come closer.

"Let me explain something to you boys," he began. "I'm a business man and a man like me gotta maintain his reputation. If one punk can get away with my money, somebody else is going to try to do the same thing. I got a business to run."

"What are you trying to say?" I asked.

"Now I know you wants to talk to him and all, but I doubt neither of us will ever see that young nigger again. You see, I gotta set an example. In our line of business we got our own *system of justice*," he said with a smile, returning to his seat at the bar and lighting up another cigar.

"I think you boys know where the door is, right?"

CHAPTER TWENTY-SIX

There was only one other person who might have some idea of Sonny's whereabouts. It was a long shot, but we decided to pay him a visit anyway before heading back to the office.

The afternoon traffic was unusually slow, which made our drive over to Park Hill an eternity. Eventually we got there and parked the squad car in front of the house. The neighbors took notice as expected. Some stood on their front porches while others peeped from behind curtains. The lock on Danita's house next door to Lester's place had been replaced and several new bright orange notices were tacked to the front door. Apparently she hadn't resolved the situation with her landlord yet. Damn.

"It's been a long time since I been in this part of town," mentioned Bobby, looking around nervously. "It ain't too safe after dark. Know what I mean?"

"Yeah," I answered absent-mindedly, knocking on the door. I knocked again after waiting for a few minutes without an answer.

"Maybe he ain't home. We can always come back later, right?" he offered, eager to leave as he took notice of the crowd forming across the street.

"He's here," I answered, not ready to give up just yet. I walked around to the back porch with Bobby reluctantly following. As expected, Lester sat rocking in his chair puffing on an old corncob pipe.

"I knows ya'll would be here sooner or later," he said quietly, looking straight ahead while still rocking. "Looks like we got us another hot day. The Lord sho is good, ain't he?"

"I guess you know why we're here."

"Yeah, I suppose I do," Lester admitted.

"And you know what's going to happen when Levi finds Sonny so let's cut to the chase. If you got *any* idea where he's headed, you better tell us now. We might have a chance of finding him before Levi's thugs do, but time's running out."

He continued to rock back and forth, slowly before answering. "Wouldn't make no sense to stay around here, now would it? I guess he gone up north somewhere. I got no idea where, but he'll make it. That boy got nine lives." He seemed convinced Sonny could just disappear. I wasn't so sure.

"Why'd you lie about the medallion?" I asked, changing the subject. He just continued to rock back and forth without saying a word.

"You either tell us what we need to know, or we can have this conversation downtown. It's your choice," I said. We were running out of time and my patience was wearing thin.

Sensing the growing frustration in my voice, Lester bent over, placed his head in both hands and exhaled. "I told that boy he was asking for trouble messing around wit that white girl. Don't matter no how now," he answered sadly.

"I'd take him along with me to Ms. Sue Ellen's place every now and then when I needed some help. I was trying to teach him how to work with his hands, seeing as how he wasn't much for school learning. He used to always see that girl over there, and I guess they got to know each other over time. Every now and then I look around and instead of working, he done run off with her somewhere around the house. Sonny Boy said they was just friends but I knows what they was doing and it was wrong. I told that boy more than once he need to be careful. You know what they do to a colored man who be messing with a white woman down here in Georgia. He was crazy bout that girl, but she was just using him to git back at that boyfriend of hers," he continued angrily.

"What happened to the girl?" Bobby shouted, jumping out of his seat and rushing over to the old man. He grabbed Lester, pulled him out of his chair and pinned him up against the back door.

"God dammit, take it easy man. This isn't the way to handle it!" I yelled separating the two and shoving Bobby back to the edge of the porch before turning my attention to the old man. I reached out to give him a hand, but he shunned the offer and slowly walked back to his rocking chair and sat down.

"You don't scare me. I bet you got a white robe and mask in the back of yo car, don't ya?" he asked Bobby, seething with anger.

"I apologize for my partner," I said, attempting to calm him down. "It's personal with him. Please, just tell us what happened."

Lester buried his head in his hands again, took a deep breath and began slowly. "He came to me one night and said he needed some money, bout two-hundred dollars. I told him I didn't have that kind of money."

"Two hundred dollars for what?" I asked.

"He said she was wit child."

"Oh Jesus!" Bobby muttered, shaking his head.

"He told me he heard there was a doctor in Atlanta that could fix that…if you know what I mean," Lester continued. "He was so desperate for money that he started working for Levi. I knows he was also hanging around wit them hoodlums on South Street, robbing people too." Suddenly this was all starting to make sense.

"The girl? What happened to her?" I asked. He didn't answer.

"Like I said, we can go downtown and have this conversation, but I'd rather not do that. I don't think you want to do that either. So it would be in your best interest to come clean now."

"Yeah, where's the girl old man!" Bobby yelled angrily, rising up from his seat again. "You hear me old man?"

He got up slowly from his rocking chair, using his cane to shuffle over to the other side of the porch. He looked out over the field where kids were playing stickball and started shaking his head.

"Life's strange ain't it? You live your whole life trying to do the right thing, but sometimes trouble finds you. Ain't right is it?" He reached in his pocket for a handkerchief to wipe away the sweat from the side of his face before continuing.

"We was just finishing up some work for Miss Sue Ellen one night when he asked me to drop him off down the road near Tipper Lake," Lester began again in a barely audible voice.

"I figured something was up, so I dropped him off at the lake, drove up the road a bit and parked. Then I walked back to where I let him out and hid in the woods. I'll never forget." He stopped and shook his head for a moment before continuing. "It was a full moon that night. The two of them was out there on the lake. They was in a canoe. Look like they was arguing bout something. But I was too far away to make out what they was saying."

"And then..." he said, pausing.

"And then what?" Bobby demanded. "And then what old man?"

"The boat, it just…it just rolled over. Now Sonny Boy, he ain't much of a swimmer but he managed to make it back to the shore, but…that girl, well…"

"You mean she…?," Bobby said, bowing his head and making the sign of the cross with his hand.

"And the body?" I asked.

"We took a canoe from their boathouse nearby and went back there out on the lake and got her body. We buried her right there in the woods at Tipper Lake."

"Do you remember where?" I asked.

"Yeah," he answered quietly. "I think I do." He was still looking out across the field at the kids playing.

"Can you take us there?"

With his head down, he nodded. We had gotten more that we had bargained for. The question now was: how were we going to handle this problematic information given the impact it was sure to have on this town?

"Miss Sue Ellen, how she doing?" Lester asked, walking back to his rocking chair and sitting down.

"She confessed to the murder of her husband. My guess is she'll probably spend the rest of her life in prison. I don't believe she did it. There's just too many loose ends that don't make any sense."

"That Miss Sue Ellen, she a good woman," he confirmed, looking directly at Bobby and me. "I feel real sorry for her, seeing what happened to her daughter and all. I believe she was in a lotta pain, not knowing what happened to her child. From then on, whenever she needed something done, I always did it for free."

"Out of guilt?"

"Yeah. I suppose you could say that," he answered.

"Were you the one who installed that furnace?" I asked.

"Yes'm."

"Were you there the night that Earl was murdered?" Bobby asked. Lester didn't answer. He had the same strange look on his face when I showed him the medallion several days ago. He started to rock again.

"Yeah, I was there that night," he said slowly. Bobby and I looked at each other without speaking. We were both surprised to hear that.

"I was there finishing up work on the furnace when I heard all this yelling upstairs. Now I'm not one to get into nobody's business, but when I seen her run out the house crying, I knew something bad had happened" he said.

"So you went upstairs to see what happened?" I asked.

"Yes'm."

"And?"

"He was lying there on the floor."

"The judge?"

"Yeah."

"Where?" I asked.

"In that girl's room," he answered. "He was trying to get up. Man had blood all over him. I tried to give him a hand you know, but he start yelling at me like I done something to him. He's screaming, 'd*on't touch me you dirty nigger*'. He say he don't want my black nigger ass in his house no more. Then he say he know that *nigger* Sonny Boy had something to do wit his daughter's disappearance." The old man paused for a moment and looked up at us with an angry glare.

"Ain't no way he coulda known what happened to his daughter, but between the police and the Klan, I think you knows what woulda happened to Sonny Boy, *even if it wasn't true.* I couldn't let that happen."

The two of us looked at each other.

"So *you* finished the job?" I asked.

"Yeah," he admitted without any remorse. "I picked up one of them dolls and I hit that son of a bitch as hard as I could, and then I hit 'em again, and again, and again!" he said angrily, going through the motion with an imaginary weapon in his hand. "Son of a bitch. And you know what, *it felt real good*!"

"And then you switched the doll dresses and set the fire to cover up the murder?" I asked.

"You call it murder, but I call it getting respect," he muttered angrily.

"I fought in World War II, the all colored 41st Battalion outta Camp Lejeune, North Carolina. Unlike you white boys, they put us on the front line in Italy. Lot of us didn't make it back home. This here limp I got come from bullet fragments still in my hip. I done paid my dues to this Goddamn country and I'm still being disrespected cause I'm colored! I'm seventy-five years old," Lester lamented, looking up at us sternly. "When do I stop being a nigger?"

I took out a Marlboro and lit up. A drink right about now would definitely be in order. I could understand his pain and frustration.

"Go inside and put your things in order. We're taking a ride downtown." He got up slowly and went inside.

Bobby began pacing back and forth from one side of the porch to the other. "We got a real mess on our hands. What we gonna do?" he asked, looking both confused and angry.

"It *is* a mess; that's for sure, but we can't let Sue Ellen go to jail for something she didn't do. We both know what the truth is going to do to this city, but we really don't have a choice. We'll have to talk this one over with the Chief."

I removed the medallion from my pocket and took another look at the inscription on the back. Why was it at the scene of the crime? Did Lester or Sue Ellen drop it, or did the Judge have it? I guess at this point it really didn't matter.

CHAPTER TWENTY-SEVEN

Several neighbors stood on their front porch while others watched from their windows as we walked Lester out to the squad car. At Bobby's suggestion, we decided not to use handcuffs. Once inside the car Bobby sat in the driver's seat while Lester sat quietly in the back.

"You all right back there?" I asked.

He looked straight ahead with a blank look on his face and nodded, yes. He seemed to have accepted his fate.

Bobby placed the radio microphone close to his mouth. "This is Car number seventy-two checking in. We on our way back to the station. We're bringing in a suspect for questioning - over?"

"Roger that," responded the dispatch officer on the other end of the line.

"Notify the Chief that we're on our way and have him meet us at the station," Bobby added before starting the engine.

"No can do buddy," replied the dispatch. "Chief just high tailed it outta here about twenty minutes ago with the DA and the Medical Examiner. Damn if they wasn't in a real hurry too," he added. "Headed over to the State Penitentiary."

"The state pen? What's going on over there?" Bobby asked him, while glaring at me.

"That judge's wife over there," he answered, "they found her hanging in her cell. Apparent suicide."

"What! You mean…Sue Ellen…is dead?" Bobby asked.

"Yeah. Damn shame, ain't it?" answered the dispatch.

"Christ Almighty!" Bobby swore under his breath.

The three of us sat there in stunned silence for the next few minutes, unable to say anything while trying to make sense of what we had all just heard.

"You still there?" asked the dispatch officer.

"Yeah," Bobby reacted slowly, voice choking. "We still here."

"You still want me to try to reach the Chief?" the dispatch officer asked. We both looked at each other, thinking the same thing.

"Naw, forget it," he answered. He took out a handkerchief from his pocket and wiped his eyes.

"Roger that," replied the dispatch officer.

I guess we were just a little too late in finally unraveling the mystery of both Catherine's disappearance and Earl's murder. Sadly, she had died never knowing what happened to her daughter and not realizing that she in fact, *had not* murdered her husband. I lit a Marlboro and sat there quietly pondering our dilemma.

"Colored boy gets white girl pregnant, girl drowns and boy's daddy kills her father. The Klan's gon have a field day wit that," said a now familiar voice from the back seat. I looked in the rear view mirror to see Aunt Doriece unbeknown to both Bobby and Lester, seating in the back seat.

"Looks like you got yo' self a real mess on your hands" she added. "You gotta do the right thing." Considering all that we now know, it would light the fuse that would rip this city apart.

I loosened my tie, took one last drag, and tossed my cigarette out the window. There was only one logical thing I *could* do.

I turned to Lester, "Get out!" He sat silently with his head down before finally looking up with a confused expression on his face.

"Did you hear what I said? Get out. Go back home!"

Bobby turned to me, stunned. "Are you crazy?" he asked, shocked by my decision.

"It all ends right here, right now."

"Meaning what?" Bobby asked, confused.

"That this stays between the three of us, *forever*! Everybody understand?" I looked directly at Bobby. "Are you prepared for the fallout if the truth gets out?" He lowered his head without answering. I knew that deep down inside he still harbored some guilt for failing to bring closure to Sue Ellen and David's daughter's disappearance. Considering the circumstances however, it made sense to quietly shut the door on this case, forever.

"What about the body?" he asked. "She deserves a decent burial."

I agreed with him, but we couldn't take the risk. I looked at him sadly, and shook my head.

"We've done the best we can do. What's done is done," I answered.

"May God rest her soul." He quietly began to weep and pray. He turned around to face Lester who sat quietly in the back seat. "You heard what the man said. Go on. Git out!"

The old man opened the back door and placed one leg out before turning to look at us.

"Thank you," he said, softly.

In a strange sort of way I was glad this was finally over. I had gotten distracted by this case against my better judgment; now I needed to focus on the real reason I was in Savannah.

CHAPTER TWENTY-EIGHT

"There's some gentlemen who'd like to speak with you," the Chief said, looking at Pete as he stood in the doorway of his office. He got up slowly from his desk and walked across the room to the office, all the while looking down and avoiding eye contact with the rest of us.

I was able to catch a glimpse of three men all wearing dark suits seated around the Chief's desk before the door closed. Today was the big day. The Feds were in town handing down sealed indictments for the illegal trafficking of narcotics, specifically hallucinogenic drugs and money laundering. My undercover investigation had exposed sixteen members of the Savannah Police Department including street cops and others involved in illegal drug activities. All in all, I had given up six months of my life to finally bring this case to closure. Unfortunately it was just the tip of the iceberg as similar trafficking of illegal drugs was also spreading to South Carolina, North Carolina, and Virginia. My assignment however was done. It was time to move on to the next phase in my career. Ironically, all the local news media turned their attention instead to the historic arrival of the *Savannah*, the world's first nuclear-powered ship completing its maiden voyage from Norfolk, Virginia to Savannah. A ship powered by nuclear energy? Sounds crazy, but most likely the first of many I'm sure and a sign of things to come.

Normally we could hear the Chief's loud voice chewing someone's ass out even with the door closed. Not today. Both Andy and Bobby sat nervously at their desks expecting to be called in following Pete. I had to display that demeanor as well to avoid exposing my cover. I requested to be indicted as well in order to protect my cover; however the charges would be quietly dropped and removed from my record.

"What you think they gonna do to us?" Bobby whispered, sweating profusely and visibly worried. I sat there silently without answering. Considering my situation, what could I say? After a moment or two he began thumbing through a small book of Bible verses and began quietly reading to himself. Expecting the obvious, Andy on the other hand was removing file folders and documents from his desk and placing them in a large cardboard box on the floor. I sat there in silence, relieved at what finally appeared to be the conclusion of this awful assignment that had taken its toll on both my patience and nerves. McKenna's murder had been an unexpected distraction that had required juggling priorities; nonetheless the primary mission had still been accomplished.

We all looked up in unison upon hearing the sound of the Chief's office door open. Pete walked out without saying a word, his head down as he headed towards the back stairway. Under his arm was a large brown envelope. Good riddance asshole. The Chief stood at the door and pointed to Andy, who slowly got up and headed into his office, shutting the door behind him.

"Twenty-five years and this is what it all comes down to?" mumbled a dejected Bobby, placing his head down on his two hands. "In my heart I knew this was wrong. You know if Erleen was still alive this woulda never happened; I would never have done this!" he lamented. Sometimes we give in to temptation for all the wrong reasons. I guess you call that being human.

"Maybe they'll go easy on you Partner," I suggested, attempting to make him feel better. "You've got a spotless record of service, otherwise. Who knows, maybe the Chief will put in a good word for you."

"I don't know. I'm in this thing pretty deep," he answered. "At the start I was only going to..."

While he continued to ramble on, I could only think about my exit from this hellhole. I had stayed here longer than expected and it was time to move on to bigger and better things. It was all about finding the right opportunity.

"Monroe. Get in here, Goddamnit!" the Chief growled, breaking my train of thought. Surprised, I got up slowly and stood at my desk waiting for Andy to exit. He couldn't have been in there more than ten minutes at most. Seconds later in much the same manner as Pete had left, he too came out carrying a large brown envelope. He stopped long enough to pick up the box of folders on the floor next to his desk and headed toward the back stairway. He never looked up or said a word.

After entering I sat in the only available chair in the room. All three agents sat next to each other on one side of the desk, while the Chief and I sat on the other side. The one sitting closest to the Chief appeared to be in charge. He did all the talking while the other two listened and constantly jotted down notes on yellow pads of paper.

To my surprise, the Chief had been aware of my assignment all along. He had certainly done one hell of job acting as if he was completely unaware of my real reasons for being here. His insistence that Bobby and me drop the McKenna investigation had me wondering whether or not he was involved in a cover up with the Mayor's office, when all along he had simply been trying to keep me focused on my primary mission.

As expected, they were interested in knowing if any other organized crime groups were involved locally in the overall operation. Although I had a hunch, that was clearly outside of the scope of my assignment. I played ignorant and stuck firmly to the information I had provided them over the last several months.

My questions on the other hand were single-mindedly focused on the timeline for getting the hell out of here. On that issue, they were somewhat vague; explaining that getting me out of Savannah was the responsibility of another office in New York.

Aware that I was on the verge of losing my temper, the Chief assured me he would personally submit a request to the Georgia Attorney General's office to expedite my reassignment. I took the Chief at his word and received my indictment just as Pete and Andy had, in a large brown envelope and was dismissed.

I exited the office and closed the door behind me before walking back over to my desk. I looked at Bobby, who nervously glanced at me.

"How'd it go?" he whispered. Suddenly the Chief's door opened. Expecting the inevitable, Bobby bowed his head and said a prayer. He stood up and began walking toward the Chief's office. As he reached the door, all three agents exited and quickly disappeared down the back stairway never saying a word or looking our way. Confused, he turned and looked at me, unable to speak before tears began to stream from his eyes.

I had purposely left his name out of the investigation and the information I turned over to the agency. Yes, he *had* made a grave error in judgment, but he had also given twenty-five years of his life to this town and in the process had lost both a son and the love of his life. He deserved to finally retire and quietly live out the remainder of his life enjoying the things he never had time for.

"What the heck is going on?" he whispered.

"Don't know," I replied, shrugging my shoulders as if I was just as surprised as he was. "Looks like you lucked out."

"What? How is that possible?" he asked.

"I wouldn't worry about it. If I were you, I'd go back to my desk and get back to work."

"What about you?" he asked, looking at the brown envelope tucked under my arm.

"Don't worry about me. I'll still be around for a little while."

He held out his hand. "If you had anything to do with this, thanks Partner. We made a great team."

"Yeah, it was good," I concluded. "You take care of yourself, and enjoy that twin-engine Chris Craft."

He gave me a big hug before walking back to his desk. Once there, he removed a file from his the desk drawer and began organizing the documents inside as usual. Just as I approached the back stairway, I turned around to take one last look at the office I'd called home for the last six months. For some reason, I wasn't as jubilant as I had expected to be at this moment that I had waited so long for.

CHAPTER TWENTY-NINE

With the federal drug trafficking case now closed, I had officially satisfied my deal with the agency. Detective Tyler Monroe was now on track to become Special Agent Tyler Monroe, G Man. I proudly straightened my silk tie in the mirror while stopping for a moment to consider what I had sacrificed to get to this moment - the loneliness of endlessly moving from one place to another, no real friends, and the emotional trauma of having to protect my real identity. The cost was certainly more than I had anticipated. At the end of the day was it really worth it? Only time would tell.

I tossed a few extra shirts in my suitcase before heading to the front door to meet Bobby, waiting outside to give me a lift to the bus station. Hopefully my trip to New York to meet the agency director to discuss my future would be a productive one.

Danita sat silently on the couch staring directly at the television set. As expected, she didn't say a word. I had known this wouldn't be easy. Although we had grown closer, I knew this moment would eventually come.

"Haven't we discussed this a million times already? Like I said, when I get settled, I'll send for you just like we planned. Okay?" Still no answer.

She was understandably upset. Did I feel guilty about leaving? Sure, but I had waited for this opportunity all my life. She continued to look directly at the television, not saying goodbye. I closed the door behind me and headed outside to meet Bobby. Once outside, I placed the suitcase in the back seat of the squad car and climbed in next to him.

"Sure you won't reconsider?" he asked, adjusting his hearing aid before shifting into gear and pulling off. "We make a damn good team." There was a little sadness in his voice.

"Did you just say damn?" I smirked while changing the radio station to something more listenable.

"I suppose it's okay to loosen up a little every now and then," he laughed, "as long as you don't forget who's in charge." He pointed to the sky.

"We do make a damn good team," I said "but it's time for me to move on. Nothing personal." We sat silently for the rest of the drive as we cut across town to the colored-only Greyhound Station.

"You sure you wanna go to this station?" he asked, looking a little confused as we approached the station.

"Yeah."

"Alright. Have it your way," he mumbled before pulling up in front of the station and turning off the engine. "Just be careful... and keep ya eyes on your suitcase."

"Don't you worry about me. I'll be fine."

"What time did you say you'll be back on Monday again?" asked Bobby.

"Five o'clock."

"All right. I'll meet ya here at five." He removed a small neatly wrapped package from his pocket and placed it in my hand.

"Take care of yourself young blood. Don't you go taking no wooden nickels, ya hear?" he said smiling. I nodded, grabbed my suitcase from the back seat and headed towards the station entrance.

As expected there was no line at the ticket counter on a Thursday evening. I had a few minutes before departing and so I decided to grab a soda and newspaper for the long trip. With any luck I would sleep most of the fourteen-hour trip. I gave the clerk seventy-five cents and shoved the change in my pocket. I glanced at the headlines as the departure gates were announced.

A small line had already started to form at Gate 12 as I approached. An old woman stood at the front of the line desperately trying to control two young kids who were fighting over a Popsicle.

"6:45PM for Washington, DC" shouted the driver standing at Gate 12 inside the bus door. "Have your tickets ready. Stops in

Atlanta, Charlotte, Richmond, and Washington DC. This is the 6:45PM to New York, Gate 12. All aboard."

At this time of the day there was a fairly small number of passengers, maybe ten at most, so finding a window seat was easy. I had a thing about window seats. Buses, trains, airplanes, it didn't matter. I *had* to sit at a window. It was probably a result of the time I spent as a child riding busses while moving from city to city.

I finished the soda, placed the empty bottle in the pouch on the back of the seat in front of me and reclined as far back as the seat would allow. Curious, I removed the package from my pocket that Bobby had given me and carefully took off its silver wrapping. It was the small white bible he always carried with him. Inside the front cover was a handwritten note:

> *Belief creates hope and hope is what gets us through the difficult times in our lives – Erleen*

Several pages throughout the bible had been folded back. On one page was a passage that had been underlined. It was Proverbs 9:10, *Fear of the LORD is the beginning of wisdom and knowledge of the Holy One is understanding.* Had Bobby marked these passages for himself or for me? Curious, I scanned several other similarly marked passages while struggling to keep my eyes open.

"Station stop, Atlanta Georgia!" shouted the bus driver, bringing a sudden and abrupt end to my unexpected nap. Strange. It seemed as if only a few minutes had passed since I had opened the Bible back in Savannah. It was 11:45PM. I picked up the Bible that had fallen on the floor and placed it back into my pocket.

"We'll be here for twenty minutes. If you want to get something to eat or stretch your legs, be sure to take your ticket with you. Twenty minutes," he warned. "If you ain't here, you get left behind. Understand?"

Nature called and I had no faith in the cleanliness of bus toilets, so I grabbed my suitcase from the rack above the seat and headed for the inside of the Atlanta station, taking notice that we were parked at Gate 7.

Atlanta was a major hub for all points north and south, so it came as no surprise to see it bustling with activity this close to midnight on a Thursday. I followed the signs to the men's restroom and took my place in a long line outside the door.

"That son-of-a bitch Governor Barnett, now that's one stinking, lying racist if there ever was one!" spouted a distinguished looking gentleman in line directly in front of me. "Who does he think he is? That idiot's making the great State of Mississippi look downright foolish. What do you think about that situation young man?" he asked, turning around and looking directly at me.

"Situation? What situation?" I asked, while looking at my watch to keep tabs on our twenty-minute layover.

"Meredith, James Meredith. Ain't you heard about the negro who's trying to attend the University of Mississippi?"

"Vaguely. I haven't really followed that too closely," I muttered, a little embarrassed.

"Damn shame if you ask me!" he said, slinging a worn leather briefcase over his shoulder and removing his glasses. "President Kennedy's ordered federal troops *and* US Marshals to escort that young man onto campus. It's an outrage. Here's a man that served his country for nine years in the US Air Force for God's sake; yet he's being treated like this. Don't you think that's an outrage?" he asked.

"I really don't have an opinion," I answered, trying to avoid being dragged into a conversation. I just needed to use the bathroom. Bad.

"No? How can you *not* have an opinion young man? Now my grandfather--God rest his soul," he interjected, "was a slave owner in Mississippi so my daddy grew up around slaves. As a boy, I remember him telling me that slavery was the most dehumanizing condition a man could ever experience. It's goes against the teachings of God Almighty, but yet here we are in 1962 and things haven't really gotten any better for the Negro."

"Why not ask for God's help?" I suggested. "From what I'm told, if you believe, then all things are possible. Isn't that right?"

"You remind me of myself as a younger man," he smiled. "Now I wasn't a religious man back then, but I did appreciate the *purpose* of religion," he continued. "Regardless of whether you're Catholic, Baptist, or whatever, the foundation of religion is *belief*, and that belief is what *inspires hope* in us as human beings. Without hope, life has no real meaning." Odd. That was the same statement Erleen had written inside the bible Bobby had just given me.

"Both Dr. King and that young man Meredith represent hope – a belief that things can change if we have faith and are willing to exercise our God-given rights and fight for that change" he continued. "This country needs more Negro role models that inspire hope in their people. They're out there," he said shaking his head, "but you might say… *they're invisible.*"

"Maybe they realize it's a *hopeless* situation," I suggested.

"Hopeless? Well if no one ever stands up to challenge the wrongs within the system, nothing will ever change. That's certainly not the way I'd want to live if I were a Negro. Would you?" Rather than answer that question, I pointed to the line in front of us that had moved closer to the men's room.

"I'm sorry. Please pardon my intrusion," he said apologetically after moving forward. "I sometimes tend to get carried away in my philosophies."

"No big deal," I replied, moving up behind him.

"Dr. Carl Stevens," he introduced himself, extending his hand. "I teach Political Science at the University of Georgia. I can tell from your accent that you're not from around these parts. Up north perhaps?" he asked.

"New York, Chicago, DC, I've been around" I replied.

"That's interesting," he said. "As a young man, I moved around quite a bit also. Had *big* dreams but never really stayed in one place long enough to make those dreams come true. In hindsight, moving from place to place was a bad thing."

"Why do you say that? I asked curiously.

"Never got a chance to settle down. I guess I was running away from the thing I feared the most…a relationship," he answered. Sounds familiar. I quickly glanced at my watch while he continued to recall his past as a young man. It was five minutes to twelve and we hadn't moved much further. Unfortunately at this point I would have to use the bathroom onboard the bus.

"Sorry to interrupt, but my bus is about to leave. It's been nice meeting you Dr. Stevens," I said

"My pleasure as well" he replied. "Remember what I said about hope," he added, his voice trailing off as I quickly made my way back towards Gate 7.

CHAPTER THIRTY

"Mr. Stuart will see you now."

I stood up, draped my raincoat over my shoulder and followed the young lady down the hall and into a large conference room. At the end of a long conference table sat an elderly gentleman, neatly dressed in a dark three-peace suit. She handed him several files.

"Will there be anything else?" she asked. He shook his head no, and pointed to an empty seat to his right before removing a pair of reading glasses from his coat. He carefully perched them on his nose and began flipping through the files without looking up as I sat down.

"Degree in Psychology, Masters in Criminology, and top of your class in Policy Academy. A spotless record. Interesting career" he said in a rather gruff voice while looking through the files. "Good work in Savannah. We needed that info badly."

"Thank you sir," I said proudly. He finally looked up.

"We're dealing with a major drug problem across this country of ours and it's only going to get worse. Good field agents like you are hard to come by, particularly those who can move around the country for months at a time." He tossed the folders on the table.

"So you want to be a G-man. Is that correct?"

"Yes sir" I answered.

"You do understand that both the training *and* commitment to this job are rigorous. Relationships and marriage – forget 'em.

"That won't be a problem, sir," I said. "I'm totally committed.

"Totally?" he asked.

"Yes sir." He stared at me silently for a moment before continuing. "And the alcohol?"

"It's under control sir" I answered.

"The next class at the Academy starts in six months at Quantico. I'm officially recommending you to be a member of that class. Until then, that's one other small thing we'll like you to take care of."

"Certainly sir" I said, with excitement.

"We're getting reports of a surge in cross burnings across the South, apparently some group that calls themselves The Pack appears to be behind this. The local law enforcement authorities typically handle things like this but there's a strong possibility that they're involved as well. We were planning to send a couple of Federal Marshals down there to investigate, but you're already on the inside so it might make more sense for you to look into that."

"But, sir..."

"You have a problem with that?" he asked, looking above the reading glasses that had slid down his nose.

"No sir" I said slowly, trying hard not to display my disappointment in having to return to the hellhole I'd just left.

"We're only talking about six months" he added, sensing my displeasure from the look on my face.

"Will that be in writing?" I asked, aware that six months could eventually turn into twelve months or more.

"If you wish" he answered finally after a few moments of silence.

"I'm going to need a few things also" I said.

"Such as?" he asked.

CHAPTER THIRTY-ONE

"Well look at you. I ain't going to ask how you got this fancy ride. I just want to take it for a spin" beamed Bobby. He opened the door and sat behind the wheel. I tossed him the keys.

"Bucket seats, overdrive transmission, a two tone paint job. Man. How much did something like this set you back for?" he asked, starting the engine. I looked down without answering.

"Sold ya soul to devil, huh?"

"Something like that" I answered.

"Well I hope it's worth it." He waited for a response. "Well, it's a good thing you called," he said, finally breaking the silence. "I was about to drive over to the bus station to pick you up. How long did it take you to drive back anyway?"

"Ten hours." He shook his head.

"You lucky you didn't get pulled over." Obviously he hadn't noticed the orange slips wedged above the sun visor. "Well, I'm glad to see you back partner, even if it's only for a few months. We got plenty of work waiting for you. In case you've forgotten, I'm outta here in a few months myself." He shut off the engine, got out and tossed me the keys. "By the way, nice haircut. You look like a human being for a change. We better get moving" he added, glancing at his watch. "Wouldn't want to be late for the Chief's morning briefing on you first day back."

We took the back entrance and hurried up the stairs to our second floor office. I placed my briefcase on the desk across from him and took a quick glance at the morning crime sheet – two stolen cars, one assault, a home invasion and a lost dog. It was a typical night by their standards.

"Monroe, Thomas...get ya ass in here right now!" shouted the six foot four figure standing in the doorway of the Chief's office. That was music to my ears. We quickly headed for his office as told.

"Shut the door and sit down," he yelled as we entered. Bobby turned to a blank page in his spiral notebook, ready to take notes.

"What in the hell are you smiling about Monroe?" he asked.

"Nothing Chief" I replied. Only six more months and I'd be out of here for good. Hopefully during that time someone would get murdered, kidnapped, or maybe involved in a hostage situation. I know that sounds terrible, but it's what I do. I love this job.

Tyler Monroe returns in

"The Pack"

CPSIA information can be obtained
at www.ICGtesting.com
Printed in the USA
BVHW01*2028050318
509754BV00004B/7/P

9 781495 140129